BY JEN BESSER AND SHANA FESTE

Dirty Diana

Diana in Love

Diana in Love

Diana in Love

A Dirty Diana Novel

Jen Besser
and Shana Feste

THE DIAL PRESS

New York

Published in the United States by The Dial Press, an imprint of Random House, a division of Penguin Random House LLC, New York.

THE DIAL PRESS is a registered trademark and the colophon is a trademark of Penguin Random House LLC.

LIBRARY OF CONGRESS CATALOGING-IN-PUBLICATION DATA
Names: Besser, Jen, author. | Feste, Shana, 1976– author.
Title: Diana in love / Jen Besser and Shana Feste.
Description: New York, NY: The Dial Press, 2024.
Identifiers: LCCN 2024015374 (print) | LCCN 2024015375 (ebook) |
ISBN 9780593447680 (trade paperback; acid-free paper) |
ISBN 9780593447697 (ebook)
Subjects: LCGFT: Novels.
Classification: LCC PS3602.E7828 D53 2024 (print) | LCC PS3602.E7828 (ebook) |
DDC 813/.6—dc23/eng/20240419
LC record available at https://lccn.loc.gov/2024015374
LC ebook record available at https://lccn.loc.gov/2024015375

Printed in the United States of America on acid-free paper

randomhousebooks.com

1st Printing

Book design by Debbie Glasserman

For Carin and Toni

Think of the long trip home
Should we have stayed at home and thought of here?

—ELIZABETH BISHOP, "Questions of Travel"

Diana
in Love

—

I like her immediately. She's tall and blond and soft-spoken. She tells me, with a smile, that her name is Brigitte. I like her made-up name and repeat it out loud as many times as I can: *Have a seat, Brigitte. What can I get you to drink, Brigitte?*

She settles into the chair opposite me and I press record.

"My fantasy is in Paris," she says.

I smile. Paris is the backdrop for so many people's fantasy. "Tell me everything."

She stretches out her legs in front of her and crosses them at the ankle. As she speaks, she pulls at the stack of brightly beaded bracelets on her wrist. "I grew up in a tiny nothing town. A town so nothing they stopped posting the population because it was dropping too fast. You pass it on a road trip and think, 'Does anyone *actually* live here?' So naturally, I fell in love with anywhere else. But really, Paris. Anything

French. I wanted to go to Paris for my honeymoon ever since I was twelve. It was the setting of an Audrey Hepburn movie I saw at my grandma's in Seguin. As we watched, she sprayed us both with French perfume to heighten the sensation that we were actually there. When I went to college, the city was a poster on my dorm room wall. My roommates had bands or movie stars smiling down on them, but I was dreaming of the Champs-Elysées. I was fascinated by the bright lights and slick rain. Paris felt like my destiny. I wondered, as I fell asleep each night, if French rain was the same texture as Texas rain.

"But then I got married, and I knew I was doomed as soon as my new husband took me to Texas Typhoon to ride waterslides instead of honeymooning in France. I guess I really knew I was doomed before that. How I chose someone so totally lacking in flavor is not something I can really explain. Even his name filled me with a quiet dread. I would be Mrs. Smith, one of millions. But we were young and he played football and liked me, so I thought I was meant to like him back. The wedding was pretty. My mama did my hair like she had done hers when she was a Rangerette. But there were all these relatives of my husband's and friends of his relatives. I'd never met half of them and I felt, from the moment I arrived at my own wedding, inspected. There's no other word for it. I walked down the aisle wearing this delicate blue-gray veil as my 'something blue.' I wanted to do something at least a little different from frilly and small-town expectations—one tiny homage to Parisian elegance so that my grandma in heaven could smile down on us.

"When I met him at the altar, his expression was flat, like I'd rolled his face with my baker's pin. He leaned in close and I thought he was going to say *You look beautiful,* but instead, in front of all those guests, he hissed, '*That's* what you're wearing?' I looked out at this sea of strangers and felt the humiliation wash over me, like a wave pulling me under, as they all stared at me. Even the wedding pictures came out wrong. My husband posed me in strange, uncomfortable positions. The same was true in bed. It was all about trying to keep him hard, and that usually meant I had to hold still, or not speak, or say things I didn't want to say, words that made me feel ugly and used. The town was shocked when he left me for a younger model he met on a weekend trip to Port Aransas. I was relieved, to be honest. I really was. I wanted to see and taste and feel and never be bland or taste anything bland ever again.

"So, in my fantasy I take up a French pen pal. Something I'd seen in my grandma's old movies. Me and this guy, we write pages and pages to each other about our lives, where we live, what we dream about. Then we start writing about what turns us on, even sharing naked pictures that I print and seal inside the envelope. And by our fifth letter, we discover a shared kink. He tells me the thing that had drawn him to BDSM is the communication. He'd recently gone through a divorce because the communication had fallen apart. They couldn't talk to each other. 'If you get into BDSM you have to say what you want, when, what your boundaries are, your "no" list, and you can't transgress or you're out of this community.' His next letter has a round-trip ticket to Paris inside and he wants nothing in return except to be disciplined. By me.

"I rush to the airport the next morning and it feels like I am making a getaway from my life. The flight is long but the second I am on it, I practice being a different person. The man at French passport control smiles at me like he knows where I'm headed and what I've agreed to do. I land to rain. Perfect, since I was already feeling myself get wet.

"In my hotel room, I impatiently watch the art deco clock, like the one Audrey Hepburn had in the old movie—only she wasn't about to meet a stranger she had agreed to treat as a submissive.

"The car arrives exactly on time, with my pen pal in it. He is even better looking in person, like an exact cross between Bond and a Bond villain. I'm glad it is so cold in Paris. It makes my nipples stand even firmer under the green satin teddy he'd had waiting for me. The black heels are higher than I'd ever worn, and when we exit for the club I almost fall on the Paris cobblestones. In my hair, I wear the most important thing, which I'd carried with me on my lap for the whole flight.

"'Do you want me to carry you the rest of the way, Mistress?'

"'You may.'

"He scoops me into his arms and I rest my head against his chest.

"Once we're beyond the velvet rope, he carries me down a blue staircase—down and down and down, me still in his arms. It takes a moment for my eyes to adjust to the darkness of the club, but all the way, I can smell a heady mix of incense and Bulgarian roses, and the lower down we go, the higher I feel.

"By the time he lays me down, I feel we must be deep in the belly of the club. I am on my back on a lush chaise lounge, the ceiling glass reflecting me back to myself. I look beautiful, more beautiful than I ever have.

"He comes toward me on his hands and knees, supplicant, worshipful, and hands me a black leather suitcase. It opens with a click. Out of all the instruments on offer to me, I choose a pearl-embossed choker and put it around his thick neck. There is something so hot about gently fixing it to his masculine lines.

"'What a pretty little bitch you are,' I tell him.

"'Thank you, Mistress.'

"He kneels, his head inches from mine as I attach a long, heavy chain to his choker. He is already panting, looking up at me, a man in his forties, but with hopeful puppy dog eyes. 'Do what I tell you,' I say. 'Yes,' he says, 'anything.' He had taken the lead at first, but now he has handed it to me, like a baton.

"His dick is the baton, protruding rock-hard. As my eyes get used to the darkness, I see I am not the only one admiring him. Now there is a crowd around us. Well heeled, beautiful bodies, and masked.

"'You turn me on so much,' he tells me.

"The people around us start to touch themselves. They are aware they are watching a performance. Women with legs spread, dipping their fingers into themselves. Men, eyes half closed, slowly rubbing their growing erections.

"'Do I please you?'

"I think about it. Does he? Am I into this? I scan my body. I look around and into the eyes of strangers who stare straight back at me. I'm swollen, thumping with desire. Yes. I tug on my pretty little bitch's hair. 'Yes?' he says.

"'Tell them to take off their masks,' I say.

"'But they need anonymity.'

"'Tell them.' My voice is harsh.

"He turns around and speaks to them. They look at one another, then remove their masks. Good. Now I can see in their faces, not just their hands rubbing themselves, not just the sound of rapid breathing, how into it they all are.

"I look up at my reflection on the ceiling. Somewhere in the distance, way up on the pavement, I can hear the rain.

"'Tell me I'm different.'

"'You're different,' he answers.

"'Tell me I'm special.'

"'You're so fucking special,' he says, crawling meekly toward my legs and spreading them. He looks into my eyes for approval, and I nod, like I am a cult leader and he is my devotee.

"'You're so special, I can taste it on you.'

"The guests move their palms faster up and down their cocks.

"Then I slap his face.

"'Can I make you come, Mistress?'

"'You don't deserve to.'

"'I'm begging you!'

"I pull the chain at his pearl collar until he is pressed again into my neck and I whisper: 'Tell me I'm never going back to that town.'

"'You are never going back to that town,' he answers.

"'Now do it!' I order, and he puts his dick in me.

"We move with the thrill of finally being bound together. We move hungrily and he begins to explore different rhythms and speeds, until I am lost in the motion with him, pulling his chain to go harder and deeper.

"'Fuck that town,' he says, and our audience claps and cheers. I'm getting closer to my edge—an edge I'd never crossed with any man before.

"'Do I have to go back?' I hear myself say.

"'Never!' He almost shouts as he fucks me so purposefully his reflection in the mirror is now a blur. 'You're free!'

"I come so hard I see stars. I see stars, like on the Champs-Elysées poster.

"I drop the chain, my limbs limp.

"I let my body shudder with orgasmic aftershocks, and he gently lifts my blue-gray bridal veil so I can study my blissed-out face in the ceiling mirror.

"I whisper something in his ear and he smiles and repeats it to me exactly as I'd told him to: 'Mistress? Do you love me?'

"'No,' I answer, 'and I never did.'"

PART ONE

Dallas, Texas

Chapter One

L'Wren pulls up to the valet outside the Hunt Gallery and we take in the chic crowd. "Who is this guy again?"

Well-dressed partygoers have spilled out onto the sidewalk. They don't look the way I had imagined they would—they're older, and if not dripping with wealth, definitely sturdy with it. "Thanks for being here."

"Of course. What are best friends for? But really, who is this guy?"

"An old friend from New Mexico," I say. "He wasn't quite this popular when we knew each other."

I fix my lipstick one last time in the mirror, my pulse quickening at the idea of seeing Jasper again. I think about all the ways I'll play it cool—Inhale: *This was a good idea.* Exhale: *This was a terrible idea.*

. . .

Jasper, the first love of my life, whom I had not seen in almost fifteen years, got in touch last week. He was in town. We met for a coffee. And it's had me rattled all week. I wasn't prepared to see him, for one thing. I thought I was meeting a business contact, a sort of blind setup arranged by my friend Alicia. When I looked up and saw Jasper, I felt like I couldn't breathe.

He was taller than I remembered, with longer legs and broader shoulders. When he sat across from me, the table and everything on it seemed to shrink. My mind raced, trying to figure out how and why he was there, right in front of me—but all my brain could conjure in that moment was a memory, from over a decade ago: the two of us lying in bed, Jasper asking if I liked the way the afternoon light fell across our naked bodies.

"Diana." Jasper's smile was warm and unhurried. "Thanks for taking the meeting." He rested his elbows on the table, his face in his hands. "Alicia and I thought it would be a fun surprise. And it seemed like a really clever idea until about a minute ago when I was standing outside and saw you through the window."

At the thought of him watching me, the tips of my ears burned. I wished I had brushed my hair this morning instead of pulling it into a messy topknot. I wished I was wearing something sexier than an old blue T-shirt of Oliver's.

"Well." I smiled. I could only laugh. There he was: deep brown eyes, dark hair, rosy lips. "It is a surprise."

I'd pictured Jasper so many times over the years, but always resisted the urge to look him up. Now that he was in front of me, I realized how uninspired my imagination had been—I'd left out all his familiar dimensions and I'd forgotten how exciting it is, the feeling, exactly, of being near a body that holds all its energy right at the surface. *Mr. Art Throb.* Those playful eyes. The smooth skin and rugged good looks.

He tipped back in his chair and crossed his arms behind his head, charisma fully intact. "I tried to call you, you know. When I got back from that first London trip. But your number was disconnected."

That was so long ago that, sitting across from him, I honestly couldn't remember if I had purposefully—while in the throes of a broken heart—changed my number when I moved from Santa Fe to Dallas, or if I was just so young and broke that I couldn't pay the bill and went without a phone for a while.

"I figured you had moved on," he said.

I noticed people noticing Jasper. A few lingering glances from other diners. He's so attractive it's comic. Sad-comic, he likes to remind you, with those sometimes-doleful eyes. "It was a million years ago."

"Fourteen. Fifteen?" he asked.

But I didn't want to go back in time. I was too excited to be with him here. Now. "How long will you be in Dallas?"

"A week, probably. I don't know." He looked up from his hands and then found my eyes. My pulse quickened. "It's nice here."

Watching him across the table, I remembered one freezing night we'd camped out in West Texas and it rained for hours. We didn't sleep at all. In the morning, groggy and shivering, I expected him to be more than ready to pack up. But he just looked at me in our cold, leaking tent and smiled. "One more night?" He could always make a terrible idea sound good. He was looking at me like that now.

We stayed like that—watching each other across the table—for what felt like several minutes, blood rushing to my cheeks, a familiar stir between my legs. The heat between us had not cooled after all these years.

"When I asked Alicia what you've been up to, she forwarded a link to the site you've been working on. Diana, as soon as I saw all your new paintings and heard your voice on those recordings, I had this swell of pride—" He stopped himself, suddenly embarrassed. "Not that I had anything to do with it, I just—"

"It's pretty wild, right?" I let him off the hook. "Sex positive. Sex obsessed? I don't know what it is yet."

"It's all that. Incredibly sexy. Beautiful, raw paintings." Jasper's phone rang then, and he excused himself. He took the call outside, pacing in tight circles, while I watched through the window, wondering if he would return anytime soon. It was a familiar feeling, waiting for Jasper. Finally, back at the table, he apologized for having to run.

"Would you come to my show's opening? It's Thursday. Here in Dallas."

My heart sank at the word *Thursday*. I wanted to see him that night. The next night. And the next. For what exactly, I didn't know. So I promised I would come to the show, and at the same time I thought, *This is not a good move. Not now. Terrible timing. He shattered your heart, remember?*

We parted minutes later, agreeing how great it was to be back in touch. We were both very polite, as if niceties could cover up any of the gaping holes we were digging with all our unsaid feelings. What do you say to a near stranger who at one point you loved more than anyone? Then we embraced and the scent of him almost made my legs give out.

Of course I spent the entire week thinking about whether or not to go to Jasper's show. What would it be like to see him now that the surprise was out of the way? And why *wouldn't* I go to see his work? Here it was, right in Dallas. I convinced L'Wren to come with me, but I haven't really told her much. And as we squeeze into the line of people waiting to enter the gallery, she falls uncharacteristically quiet.

"L'Wren?" I let her name hang like a fully formed question. I squint into the late-afternoon sun looming just over her shoulder, then add, "Tell me."

"It's nothing. Honestly." Her eyes dart from me to her sandals and back to me. "I was just thinking . . . Kevin told me he heard that Oliver wasn't seeing that lady from the food court anymore."

I've spoken to Oliver very little since he moved out and seen him even less. The last time he dropped off our daughter, Emmy, at my house, a woman was sitting in the front seat of his car. She sat the way I imagine a new girlfriend would—smiling politely, sunglasses still on, a gentle wave in my direction, but nothing to make too big a show of her presence. She had a wide smile with lots of white teeth and pulled off a pixie cut in a way that makes other women believe they, too, could pull off a pixie cut. And while she could very well be an astro-physicist or an Olympic swimmer, because L'Wren had heard a rumor that Oliver met her at the mall, and in allegiance to our friendship, L'Wren refers to her exclusively as "that lady from the food court."

"And so I just wanted to make sure you had all the facts," L'Wren insists. "About Oliver being single."

I study her expression, her mouth turned down in a slight frown. Does she think it's a good thing or bad thing that Oliver is single? Before I can decide, she changes the subject entirely. "I've always wanted to come here." The line moves forward and she loops her arm in mine, smiling. "Trish's husband claims he bought a Seok here for over a hundred K. Your mystery guy must be fairly well known."

"He's not my guy."

"Can I make him my guy?" A picture of Jasper in the gallery's window welcomes partygoers. He looks just like he did at the café—all dimples and easy charm.

As soon as we enter, L'Wren runs into a couple she knows from her club and I slip away, steadily working my way through the gallery, staying alert in case Jasper should suddenly appear. I glance around the room. He should be quick enough to spot, a crowd of admirers buzz-ing around him.

When he's nowhere to be seen, I decide to make a slow lap and take in the show. It's easy to get sucked in. Jasper's photographs are commanding, making you want to hold their unflinching gaze. A woman alone on what looks like desert sand newly soaked in rain; a young boy's narrow face in the window of a crumbling villa. The show is more varied than the last one I'd seen, especially with the mix of landscapes and portraits.

When I don't see Jasper in the crowd, I pull out my phone and send him a text.

Walking through your show right now. It's gorgeous.

I don't expect a response—maybe he's being feted before he arrives fashionably late—but I keep my phone in my hand anyway just in case. I move through the crowd, where it's deepest near the bar, and there is something comforting about being swallowed up by it. I slip into its stream and we move like a school of fish from one photo to the next—until, near the window, a black-and-white photo catches me by surprise. It's me, a younger me, sitting at Jasper's kitchen table, my face angled away from the camera. I'm naked, except for a pair of white socks, holding up a treat for the dog who is leaping into the air.

My feet feel stuck, even as the floor beneath me drops. My heart races and I close my eyes so the room will stop spinning. I pull myself here, back to this gallery and this crowd, and far away from that kitchen. As if on cue, Jasper texts back.

Don't be mad. No one will know.

I turn, expecting to see him behind me, watching me.

But he's not here. I scan the crowd again. A short brunette dressed head to toe in cream-colored Chanel and her bored-looking partner. A man with orange-tinted glasses whispering into his cell phone, his hand cupped over his mouth. Three women with matching cocktails chatting, barely looking at the photographs. I keep searching. I look for Jasper's familiar posture when he's in conversation, the way he always leans into the person speaking or crosses his arms when he laughs politely. When I don't see him anywhere, I quickly text: *Are you here?*

His reply is instant.

Sadly, no. I was needed last minute in Berlin.

I feel the adrenaline leave my body, relieved he can't see me, blushing in front of my own photo. But after the relief, a wave of disappointment. My phone chimes again:

It's my favorite in the entire collection. It reminds me of you.

Because it IS me? And so he doesn't think I'm upset by the photo, I add: *Naked in a gallery full of strangers . . . ?*

Well. Yes. I suppose I could take another one of you in a turtleneck and slacks? But it won't be as good.

A heat returns to my cheeks and doesn't stop there. It travels into my throat and down the length of my body. I feel an overwhelming desire to be in Jasper's presence, for his arms to wrap around me from behind and for him to hold me like he used to, my head resting against his chest.

I have to know. I'm guessing Dallas isn't your next stop after Berlin?

London. Then Paris. Back to Berlin. Then maybe?

After a pause he adds: *A nice kitchen table somewhere?*

I smile. Trying to figure out what to write. Overwhelmed that I'm standing in the middle of his work. It makes me miss him so much.

Germany is cold, he types. *I could use your warmth.*

I stand in the shadow of his photograph, looking up at the girl in her socks and remembering the boy who broke her heart. The way he left town, left us, just when we were getting started. Sobered by the memory, I reply, *It's a beautiful show, Jasper.*

Before I can decide if I should add more, L'Wren is at my side. "Is that *you*?"

I take in her eyes, growing wider. "We can get going."

"I knew it was you! You look insane. Look at your legs."

"We should go." I swallow but I can't seem to catch my breath. The room is suddenly small and way too warm.

"Hey. It's okay." L'Wren takes my sweaty palm. "Let's get you some fresh air."

She leads me up to the roof where it's mostly empty, except for a bar with no line and a group of men in tidy suits, deep in conversation. L'Wren offers me water and squeezes my shoulder. "You okay?"

"Jasper's my ex."

"I put that together, hon," she replies with a laugh.

When I get home, I listen to a message from Oliver. He's canceling on me for dinner tomorrow night, a dinner we've already rescheduled three times in the weeks since he moved out. *I'm just not feeling up to it after all.*

I take a shower and get into bed, and then I do what I've done every night since Oliver moved out—I lie awake for hours, unable to fall asleep. I replay the exchange with Jasper in my mind, while trying to convince myself that not seeing him tonight was *fine.* Of course he's busy, he's got a full life and so do I. So much time has passed since Santa Fe. We don't really know each other anymore. Maybe I'll see him again, maybe not.

I do see him again. When I finally drift off, Jasper appears in my dream. We're in a room with blindingly bright light and I'm asking him if we can close the drapes.

As soon as he does, the room comes into sharp focus. The walls are painted a pale blue and I don't recognize anything about the place. There's a bed and a chair and a rug that's too small for the room, and I hear myself say out loud, "Don't get too caught up in the details," even though I meant only to think it, silently, to myself.

Jasper laughs and pulls me close. He's not wearing a shirt, just jeans, and his bare chest is warm against mine. Otherwise, he looks exactly as he did at the café. And the flush that washed over me when I saw him there returns—this time with a crushing intensity.

I'm not wearing a top, only a black skirt and a bra that's lacy and pink and unfamiliar. When Jasper unclasps it, I'm relieved to feel it slip from my shoulders and fall onto the floor. I want to feel his hands on my naked breasts.

"Jasper." I mean it to be a warning, for both of us—we shouldn't be here, something is telling me it isn't allowed. But instead, it sounds like exactly what it is: a plea. Asking him to touch me everywhere, all at once.

"Why did you come up to my hotel room?" he asks.

This is his hotel room? There's nothing on the walls, no paintings, no photographs, even the bed has only one blanket and no pillow.

"Why are you here?" he asks again, this time whispering in my ear.

He runs his fingers down my arms and I shudder. "I don't know. Maybe it was a mistake?"

"Then why are you still here? Why not leave?"

When I don't answer, Jasper traces the waist of my skirt until he finds the zipper. His hand stops there, but he steps closer, only inches from me. "You still . . ." He looks into my eyes. "You still have this hold over me." He unzips my skirt and it drops to my ankles. I'm completely naked now. He takes a step back and takes me in, sucking in his breath. The floor bends under my feet, a familiar unsteadiness, like the ground may buckle. Then a voice in my head: *Keep him here. Hold on to him.* I reach for his belt loop and pull him toward me.

"I really should go. I'm so late." I breathe in the space between us and let it warm my entire body.

"Stay a little longer . . ."

"No," I whisper. But I'm still not moving. I can't.

Jasper tilts my chin up and kisses me, slowly, his lips warm against mine. The floor beneath my feet is carpeted now, soft and plush. "Stay with me," he whispers. "Don't go. Please."

The sound of his pleading sends waves of pleasure through me. I take a small step away so I can unbutton his jeans. He moans with anticipation as I pull them down, then slowly take him in my hand. He grows in my palm. And I feel more alive than I have in months.

"Get down," I say, pushing him onto the floor.

"Diana," he moans and does as I say. I watch him lie down, but I stay just out of his reach. "Please," he says again. I don't let him touch me. Instead, I circle him, taking in his body while he takes in mine. The room grows even darker, but it feels welcome—it's just the two of us, alone, and the dimmer the room gets, the smaller it feels, bringing us closer and closer together.

I sit on the edge of the bed and open my legs. He moans again, and I watch as he strokes himself.

"Don't touch," I tell him. "Just watch." He obeys, pulling his hand from his erection. "Good."

I spread my legs wider so he can see how swollen I am, how much I ache to be touched. He reaches for me again, but I bat his hand away. "Only me." His hand falls back to the floor beside him. When he settles, I slip two fingers inside me, then close my eyes, pleasure coursing through me. I lie back on the bed, moving my fingers deeper and faster, lifting my hips slightly off the bed, tightening my thighs against my hand. When I open my eyes, Jasper is standing over me. I take his hand and a current passes through us. We both smile at the familiar electricity of our touch.

"I missed you," he says.

"I'm here."

"Can I touch you now?" I take both of his hands and pull his body onto mine. "Diana," he whispers into my mouth, and I respond by kissing him deeply, then pushing him onto his back.

As I straddle his waist, the room spins. All I want to do is fall into him and steady myself. But I'm afraid if I do, he'll disappear. I stay sitting up and I let him touch me. First I give him permission to squeeze my hips, then my ass. Then I move his hands to my breasts. He props himself on his elbows so he can take my nipple in his mouth. His lips are warm and full and I don't want him to ever stop kissing me.

I throw my head back and cry, "Oliver." Fuck. The wrong name hangs heavy and loud in the room. I can't take it back.

Jasper looks up, surprised, then smiles. "Is that who you want me to be?"

The room grows darker still, so dark that he can't read my distress. "No. I just want it to be us." I close my eyes and will the room to remain the same, for us to stay just like we are.

In answer, he lifts me by the hips and glides himself inside of me. I'm flooded with heat and desire and the feeling of him deep inside of me. We move against each other, something building that neither of us wants to end. The closer we get to climax, the lighter the room gets, until we come together, the sun bright and hot.

I open my eyes. I recognize the room I'm in. Every detail is overwhelmingly familiar. The walls are painted the exact shade of white that Oliver and I debated for weeks; the shutters are the same ones we hung four years ago, when we had enough extra money saved; the sun streaming through them is at the exact angle of every late-spring sunrise, and the pieces of sky I can see wear their usual wash of yellow and orange.

But most familiar is the sensation, an old one that comes rushing back—the feeling of waking up content and satiated after sex with Jasper.

Chapter Two

—

Two days later, I squeeze myself into the back seat of L'Wren's Range Rover, wedged between Halston's empty booster seat and an impressive basket of kid snacks—animal crackers, fruit tape, and several tiny, neglected boxes of raisins. L'Wren sits in the passenger seat up front while her husband, Kevin, drives. I sit behind him, his seat pushed so far back that I have to angle my knees diagonally to fit.

Late last night, on impulse, I texted Jasper. I told him again how much I enjoyed his show. It was one sentence, which I typed and re-typed four times.

Then I spent an embarrassing amount of time trying to decide whether to add an *xx*. In the end, I left it off and hit send. I slipped my phone onto the nightstand and told myself it would be tomorrow before I heard back.

But his reply was instantaneous:

I guess because we missed seeing more of each other in Dallas, you'll have to come visit me in London.

Then a pause—three dots appearing, then disappearing, while my heart pounded—before he added:

Must be late for you there.

I will my fingers to move quickly, as if my typing could somehow convey the kind of nonchalance I can't actually muster. *Couldn't sleep. Lots of insomnia these days.*

Uh-oh. I've rubbed off on you.

It read like an invitation to be dirty.

Didn't it? I don't overthink it, just type:

It's true.

Three dots appear, then disappear. Once. Then twice. Then:

Good night, Diana. xx

To say I haven't been checking my phone all day and, worse, thinking about flying to London, would be a massive lie.

"Who are you texting back there? Bet I can guess!" L'Wren calls from the passenger seat. Kevin shoots her a *be quiet* look. He's on a conference call over the car's speaker that we're all forced to listen in on. In just under two minutes I've gathered: The guy on the other end of the call is named Howie; Howie is very disappointed with a guy named Jeremy's lack of transparency; Kevin's job seems very boring.

"No one," I whisper from the back seat. No new messages. I slip my phone back into my purse.

L'Wren ignores Kevin's warning. "I have Capri Sun, hon, if you're thirsty?"

I shoot her a thumbs-up and grab a fruit punch. I try to quietly unwrap the straw as Kevin tells Howie he'll "circle back next week."

"You got it, bro," Howie says before hanging up.

L'Wren rolls her eyes. "Ugh."

"What? Howie's a good guy."

"He's a weenie. And he shouldn't be calling anyone *bro*. Ever."

"That weenie-bro paid for this car."

"That defense is getting *so* tired. Diana, we should start a new drinking game—every time one of Kevin's bros says 'guardrails' or 'pain point,' we drink."

"You're adorable." Kevin sighs and squeezes her knee.

"Is this weird?" I pipe in from the back. "Me tagging along with you guys?"

"There is no *right* way to do this, Diana. We're happy to all go together. Right, Kev?"

"Absolutely. I love it when my wife's best friend crashes date night." L'Wren swats his shoulder. "Ow. I'm kidding." Kevin looks at me in his rearview mirror and smiles. "And yes, going to a school musical is considered a hot date these days. That's apparently where we are."

"Oh my god." L'Wren turns to face me. "We have date nights all the time. Kev just works right through them so they're more like meetings."

"When was the last time we had a real date?"

"Maybe if *you* planned them instead of assuming I'd do it on top of my ninety other to-dos."

"Hear that, Diana? I'm a to-do!" His tone is light and cheery, but I still want to get us off this rocky terrain.

"Well, don't take marriage advice from me, am I right?" It's supposed to be funny but lands with a thud. Kevin makes a slow left into the parking lot while I blather on. "You guys are supposed to give *me* advice is what I meant. Like when we get inside, do I save a seat for Oliver? Or do I assume we sit apart? *Should* we sit apart? If he's already there, do I see if he's saved me a seat or just grab the first seat I see?"

Since Oliver moved out I've kept comically busy. I've spent hours volunteering at Emmy's school: I've shelved books in the library, designed the school's end-of-year-picnic T-shirt, collected money for the teachers' gifts, and yesterday I replied enthusiastically to an email about fitting in a recorder concert before the end of the year, for which I will organize refreshments on my own, no problem.

At work, I keep my head down, trying not to think too long about the fact that I'm still employed by my father-in-law, despite being separated from Oliver. I also try to avoid wondering about what my co-workers think of me being there, which means I avoid the office kitchen and too many trips to the mailroom, copier, or bathroom.

On evenings when the calendar is empty, I go to bed early, only to fail hard at falling asleep. Eventually I give up and pad down to the kitchen, the floorboards creaking under my feet. *I'll buy a new rug,* I think, *to drown out this awful sound. Do they make those—rugs to cure your loneliness?* I pour myself a bowl of Emmy's cereal and turn on the TV. My program of busyness is a failed experiment. I'm tired but not sleeping. And the sadness and confusion over separating from Oliver still creeps in.

L'Wren can see I am lost in my thoughts. She reaches into the back seat and squeezes my hand.

"Diana. It's a first-grade sing-along and Emmy will be thrilled you're both here. Just, you know, be in the moment."

"She's right," Kevin agrees. "Let it happen organically."

Organically was not a Kevin buzzword until last month when L'Wren sent him on a "wellness retreat" because he works too much—even in semiretirement—and she's afraid he's going to drop dead of a heart attack from the stress. "It happens," she would often repeat.

On the first day of the retreat they confiscated Kevin's phone, and for the next three days he studied his chakras and "ate seeds," he said. But then he came home praising L'Wren for adding five years to his life. He scattered rose quartz crystals around the house, bought raw nuts in bulk, and started blending his own hemp milk. L'Wren was relieved he was taking care of himself. Until the next week when she heard him on a series of conference calls, closing a deal to franchise the wellness center. When I reminded her, "At least he's driven, right?," she gave me a sad, tight smile.

"You're right. Let it happen." I unbuckle my seatbelt. "It's just that we haven't both gone to the same school function since he moved out. We split up Emmy's soccer games and activities—"

Kevin sighs, wistful. "I wish *we* could do these things apart . . ." He pulls into a parking spot, then spies an even better one and reverses.

L'Wren pretends to be offended. Or maybe she really is. I try to read her posture as she admonishes him. "So you could stay home while I go and listen to 'This Little Light of Mine' performed for the three hundredth time?"

"Heck, yeah." He turns off the car and kisses his wife on the cheek. L'Wren smiles, her shoulders relaxing, and a potent mix of envy and loneliness rolls through me. I look down at my flats, pretending to gather my purse so I don't tear up. Tears come so easily lately. I blame the insomnia. It's not like this experience is anything new—I've always noticed, being around L'Wren and Kevin, how they bicker and then easily forgive, how their annoyance or disappointment always seems to dissipate so quickly. Whenever Oliver and I disagree, it's like the tension can never evaporate. It takes over the whole mood, the entire room, hanging over us thick and stifling.

Inside the school auditorium it smells like Lysol and little kid sweat, and seats are filling up fast. "Do you see Oliver?" I keep my eyes glued to L'Wren and avoid looking for him myself. "Is he already here?"

"Jesus, Diana. He's not the Rock. Just beware the Hat Lady."

"*Raleigh*." I remind her of the name of the fellow school mom Oliver slept with, even though I know she knows it perfectly well.

"Mmm." L'Wren presses her lips together. "She'll be 'the Hat Lady' till she takes her last conniving breath."

We find a half-open row and sit, an empty seat beside me. "Should I put my bag here? Just in case?"

"Oh my god. Diana." L'Wren laughs. "Put the bag on your head if you want. You are seriously overthinking this."

Jenna's blond curls bound straight toward us. "It's a literal wall of body odor backstage with the sixth graders." L'Wren's friend since high school, Jenna makes a big show of inhaling, her nostrils vibrating. "I can finally breathe. Can they not smell themselves? Y'all know what's strange? Brooksie's body odor actually smells like his dad's. It's so bizarre. I wonder if that means Alice's will smell like mine? Oh my god"—she looks over my shoulder—"Oliver. Eleven o'clock."

"Subtle, Jenna," L'Wren scolds.

"Is he alone?" I whisper.

"All by himself. Are you saving that seat for him? What's the plan?"

"No." I rest a tentative hand on my purse.

Jenna straightens. "Got it. Good. Let him sit in the nosebleed section with the caregivers. Am I right?"

The houselights flicker on and off to let us know it's time to take our seats. Jenna balls her fists. "Crumbs! I gotta go hairspray some third graders."

As soon as Jenna disappears, I place my purse on the empty seat to reserve it.

"Thanks for saving me a seat." Oliver rushes into our row and I almost don't recognize him. There are no awkward apologies as he makes his way to us, stepping over annoyed parents. He moves quickly and confidently as if gracing the auditorium with his presence. "Sorry I'm late." He lowers into the seat beside me. "I lost track of the miles." He's freshly showered, his hair still wet.

"How far did you run?"

He checks his watch. "Nine and a half."

"Miles?" I think of how often Oliver used to melt into our couch and how much time he'd spent there. Sometimes while watching TV, he would sink so far into the depths of the cushions that I had to pull him up with both hands.

The houselights dim completely and the kindergartners are

herded onto the bleachers onstage, where soon they are busy staring into the audience, searching for their moms and dads and bumping into the little bodies in front of them. Oliver smiles at me, eyebrows raised—a familiar look that says, *here we go.* Usually I dread how long these performances are, but sitting next to Oliver feels good, as if I were the one who'd just gone for a brisk run.

A mop-headed kindergartner in head-to-toe denim takes center stage. He opens his mouth and belts the opening of "You've Got a Friend in Me" with the voice of an angel. With every note he hits, my nerves for Emmy triple. Singing is not her gift.

Oliver leans in close, a worried look on his face. "Do you remember caroling with Emmy last year? She was so confused when people would back away midchorus . . ."

"I'm still scarred. Her class is up next . . ."

The woman in front of us turns her head, whipping her ponytail to register her annoyance with our talking. As Emmy takes the stage, a nervous, giggly feeling rises in me. Oliver and I don't dare look at each other as the first graders sing "Happy." Emmy keeps her eyes on her teacher just in front of the stage, smiling big and following the teacher's every cue. I relax, my body finding the back of my chair for the first time since she'd taken the stage. But then, near the end of the song, Emmy takes a step forward, moving to the front row of the bleachers, then onto the stage floor, as if to separate herself from her peers.

"Her voice is really cutting through, isn't it . . ." Oliver whispers.

"It is."

"What is she doing with her arms?"

I shake my head. "She's gone rogue."

Emmy hits a high—too high—note and Oliver reaches for my thigh, squeezing nervously.

"This is your fault, really," I tell him. "She has your mother's voice."

"My mother sounds like Eleanor Roosevelt."

I snort, I can't help it, and this time the ponytailed woman shushes us.

This only makes it worse, both of us trying not to laugh and failing.

L'Wren leans into us. "What is going on here, friends? Huh? Got the giggles?"

I clear my throat and look straight ahead, tears quietly streaming down my face. From the corner of my eye, I see Oliver purse his lips together, showing the same determination. The song ends and the audience claps. This is good. We're going to make it out of here tonight without getting in any more trouble.

And then the stage lights dim and the spotlight finds Emmy.

"Oh no," Oliver exhales. And I lose it, Oliver's genuine panic tipping me over the edge. The piano teacher starts playing "True Colors" and my shoulders heave while I bite down on the inside of my cheek. *Donotlaughdonotlaugh. You cannot laugh while your daughter sings,* which is exactly why we cannot stop laughing. Beside me, Oliver covers his mouth and I swear I hear him hiccup, like a choked giggle gone wrong. And then, in the dark auditorium, we clasp hands.

We squeeze each other's hands and will a kind of calm into each other. We make our faces go stone-cold sober while listening to Emmy sing her heart out, never hitting a single right note.

After the show, Oliver and I mill on the empty stage with L'Wren, waiting for Emmy and Halston to change.

"What do we say?" I ask.

"Compliment the process," Oliver says, quoting from a parenting book we skimmed but never read years ago.

He opens his arms wide as Emmy jumps into them. "Can I sleep over at Halston's? We're going to do the whole show again!"

L'Wren doesn't miss a beat. "Girls. I love that. But *even better,* let's hold the show in our hearts." She holds a hand to her chest. "Forever in our hearts."

"We want to do the show again for Daddy!" Halston pipes in, hopping from one foot to the other. "He was sleeping, I saw him."

"Daddy?" L'Wren feigns surprise. "No, no. He did rest his eyes, maybe for a few seconds, and then he popped right back up."

We follow Halston's gaze into the audience, where the seats have emptied and Kevin is napping, his head tipped up to the ceiling, his mouth slack.

L'Wren leans into me and whispers, "Kevin owes me *so big* . . ." And then to the girls, she chirps, "Let's go, ladies! Wake up Daddy on the way out! Oh wait, Diana." She stops downstage. "Am I your ride?" She looks from me to Oliver.

"I can drop her," Oliver offers, and I feel a rush of excitement.

We watch them go, gathering Kevin on the way out, the auditorium doors shutting with a loud thud behind them. The theater is truly empty now, performers scattered to their cars, the lucky ones heading out for long-promised ice cream. This time last year, Oliver and I would have driven home together and likely drifted to our separate corners of the house, saying good night to Emmy but not to each other.

"You aren't hungry, are you?" Oliver asks. His voice echoes through the empty auditorium.

"Starving."

Oliver drives us to a restaurant we haven't been to since before Emmy was born. An upscale pub with overpriced food and imported beers and a pool table in the back. He took me here when we were first dating, I assumed because it was so dark inside no one would really notice if we were making out. But he was a perfect gentleman all night.

Sitting across from him now, both of us sipping an expensive whiskey, I remember the panic I felt so many years ago, when a waiter brought the menu and I skimmed it for anything I could afford. On each of our early dates, I would insist I only wanted water to drink with my steak and Oliver never questioned me. On his way to the restroom he would slip his credit card to the waiter, and when he returned to the table he would tell me the bill had been comped. "Turns out the owners are old family friends," he'd say, or something similar. I would pretend not to notice he'd paid, and we kept up like this for a while, until my paycheck caught up with his and I could slip my card to the waiter.

Tonight, I order a citrus salad to start and calamari for us to share and a steak sandwich for myself. When the food comes, we dig in like we haven't eaten for days. "It tastes just as good," I say between bites.

"Of course it does." Oliver takes a drink. "It's the Fitz."

"This was our favorite. In the beginning."

"And now look at us." Oliver's tone is perfectly neutral—he could easily mean *look at us now, still in each other's lives after so many years.*

Or, *look at us now, sitting so close but having drifted so totally apart.*

"Yeah, look at us." I match his dispassionate tone and then raise him one, forcing a lightness into my voice. "Two proud parents of a smart, beautiful kid who can be anything she wants to be when she grows up. Except a vocalist. Or perhaps anything involving music. Or rhythm, most likely."

When Oliver laughs, my shoulders relax. He doesn't want to wallow either. *Look at us now.* "You look good," I tell him. "The running. It's working for you."

"You look good too. Whatever you're doing."

"I mean it. Your spirit is back." There's a noticeable glow to Oliver's skin, and even his smile seems wider somehow. I want so badly to ask what he's been thinking, what his plan is. Where is he going to work? Have any of his interviews been promising? But I'm afraid any questions about the future will ruin the mood.

"I'm happier, that's for sure." His voice is quiet, and I lean close without meaning to. "Sometimes I think, honestly, I don't know how you put up with me for so long. Walking around with a black cloud over my head. I owe you a thank-you. If we hadn't separated, I'm not sure I would have made these changes."

"Quitting your job?"

"All of it."

"Oh. Well. Not every change has been good."

Oliver takes another sip of his whiskey. "It's strange, isn't it? Doing all this without each other."

"It is strange." Tears prick the back of my eyes and I blink quickly, trying not to cry.

"Oh, Diana." He reaches for my hand across the table. "Please don't."

I close my eyes. I refuse to ruin the evening. Under the table, with the hand Oliver isn't holding, I pinch my thigh until the red-hot discomfort is enough to distract me. I don't want to cry at the table. I don't want this evening to slip into sadness. But I can see the hurt on Oliver's face—and I can't tell anymore, is it his hurt or mine that he's wearing? Does it matter? And I lied, the food isn't as good. The salad is soggy and the calamari is chewy, like it's been in a deep freezer for too long. I shift in my seat and remember, too, how uncomfortable these chairs have always been, with their dulled leather cushions.

Oliver squeezes my hand. "We can't cry at restaurants. It's too sad. That can't be us."

"Okay," I say, but this only makes my tears spill faster. "I can't help it, if you're nice to me, I'll only cry harder." He hands me his napkin to wipe my eyes and a sob catches in my throat. "See?" My *I told you so* makes us both give a kind of strangled laugh.

"Just breathe," he says, and I do. Deep, slow inhales.

"Another drink? We could close the place down." It's barely nine, but the restaurant is emptying. There's only a sallow-faced man in a plaid shirt, alone at the bar. The light above our table is flickering, the music is too croon-y, and it smells like stale beer and chewy calamari.

"No." I shake my head. "I'd like to go home."

"Okay, let's." The way he replies, so resolutely, surprises me—like he's accepting an invitation. "Yeah."

I stop in the restroom and blow my nose and wipe my runny mascara while Oliver pulls the car around. When I step outside, he opens the car door for me, like he used to do, on all those early dates. On the ride home, I watch the road ahead, trying to figure out how to feel. Does Oliver think he's coming inside the house with me? Does he want to? Do I want him to? My eyes are hot from crying so I close them and roll down my window, listening to Spoon on the radio and feeling the wind on my face. When I open them again, Oliver is watching me. His gaze moves slowly back to the road. He's easy. I can't remember him ever being so easy.

At the house, he parks the car and comes around to open my door. On the front steps, we stop, his arm brushing my shoulder. If I take out my keys, will it break the spell? I don't have to find out. Oliver reaches into his pocket and pulls out his own set of keys. Of course he has house keys—for a moment I feel so relieved, so warm inside, just at the thought of not being the only adult who lives here. It's a grounding sensation like my feet are making more contact with the earth, like the house, too, is more solid, and I don't have to worry anymore about it blowing away or falling in on itself. Oliver unlocks the door. I follow him inside. Neither of us says a word.

I shut the door behind us and immediately we're kissing. His hands cup my face and his lips are warm and soft and taste like whiskey. My arms are around his waist, pulling his body closer to mine. He feels so solid under my touch. We stay like this, kissing in the entryway for what feels like hours. In between kisses, we confess "I missed you."

Over the last couple of years, I have slowly built a wall between us without knowing why. Maybe I'm too afraid to ask what I'm protecting myself from. Was it Oliver's depression I was so afraid of? Was it my own? Now at night when I can't sleep, I wonder if I've been too afraid to stare deeply into our marriage only to find it's unfixable. Our intimacy was once a deep pool and then it dried up. I didn't want to acknowledge how dangerously shallow it had become. I didn't care why or who was to blame, I only cared that we wouldn't be able to fix it and I was too scared to admit it. But tonight the wall feels more like a wooden fence; and the fence feels weak and clumsy, built from twigs and stupidity, held together with bubble gum and pointless resentments.

Oliver's tongue is in my mouth. He pulls me into him without hesitation, with urgency. He feels familiar but exciting, a toy I had lost then magically found.

My entire body swells with desire. This is not Oliver from just six months ago. We shed those versions of ourselves, and now we have this. This lingering spark.

He moves quickly to pull off my shirt and unclasp my bra, letting it fall to the floor. His hands cup my breasts. "Diana." He grabs my hair and pulls my head back, kisses my neck and tells me he likes the way I taste.

I take off my jeans, then my underwear. He watches me, his eyes going wide. "Let's go." He scoops me up and carries me up the stairs, his arms strong around me. At the top, he puts me down. We can't keep our hands off each other.

"Your body is different," I say.

"Yeah?"

"You're different."

"It's still me." I catch something like sorrow in his voice.

"No, it's good," I say. I don't want anything but this good feeling for both of us.

He smiles and his hands are all over me, searching me with confidence. I try to return his conviction, pushing him onto the floor beneath us, just outside our bedroom door. I climb on top of him and spread my legs so he can feel how aroused I am. He groans in pleasure as the tip of his cock connects with my wetness. "Diana," he says again.

I take the shaft of his penis in my hand, slowly gliding it between my thighs, back and forth against the softest part of me, over and over again. His breath is shallow, and I draw out the moment for as long as I can.

"Kiss me," he commands. We haven't kissed like this in so long. Really kissed. I suck on his lower lip and then let my tongue circle his, over and over again. We kiss like this until his stubble starts to burn my chin, and when I break away he moans even louder. He pulls my hair back and my mouth opens wide, almost in surprise, and he presses his tongue inside me again. We are seconds away from sex, and all I want is for him to be inside me. All of him. In all of me. I slowly circle my pelvis, massaging the head of his erection, both of us on the edge.

"Let's make it to the bed." We move together across the bedroom floor, my body still on top of his.

We make it as far as the foot of the bed before he rolls on top of me. "More," he says in my ear. "I want more."

And for a moment, we stay like this. Kissing more deeply, my pelvis pressed into his, the tip of his erection teasing me.

And then, something shifts. It happens so quickly. A murmur from the air-conditioning vent, a creak from the attic somewhere—the familiar background noises of our house. A symphony we know by heart. I don't know if it affects him first or me or both of us together. It's as if someone has just turned on the lights too quickly and we're both left squinting at our naked bodies. Our kisses grow cold and damp—because here we are in our bedroom, the setting of too many unresolved fights, heavy with the ghostly sensation of being so lonely despite lying next to someone else.

Oliver sits up first. "I'm sorry."

"Me too."

"I let it go too far." He pulls me up and we perch on the edge of the bed, our bare feet on the floor.

"I did too," I say. "We both let it go too far." Tears burn hot behind my eyes and again I blink quickly to hold them back. We've been gaslit by our own past and now our bodies are like snakes, still twitching with life after our heads were cut off.

"Hey . . ." He squeezes my knee.

"It feels so sad all the time, Oliver. Will it always feel so sad? Being apart? What if we're doing the wrong thing?"

"Well, I'm no genius, but I'm guessing this . . . is not exactly right." I glance at our naked bodies, his penis soft between his legs.

"What do we do next?"

"I don't know. But I don't think we have to dissect it tonight."

"When?" I feel the embarrassment of us taking it too far and the rising panic of being stuck in a loop. "We never talk about what's next. I need to talk to you about real things."

Oliver looks toward the bedroom door, as if scanning the room for his clothes and an easy getaway.

"If we can't talk honestly at this point . . ."

"It is sad." He looks me in the eye. "I'm sad. It's not the same. And this, tonight, is a Band-Aid over a bullet hole."

He's right, which makes it so hard to hear. I grab for a blanket to cover my naked chest. "So, now . . ."

He shrugs. "We admit that Band-Aids won't work. Despite how good we could make each other feel for a little while."

"Right." In my mind, I hear him say, *We stay here all night long and hold each other. When we get sad, we hold each other tighter,* even though I'm not totally sure it's what I want him to say.

"And I should probably go."

"Probably."

He takes my hand and the kindness of this gesture makes me well up. "Diana. I'm so sorry we can't seem to figure this out."

"I'm sorry too. I keep doing that. Apologizing after you do."

He kisses my cheek and stands.

"Oliver?" I'm flooded with the memory of the last time he left.

When we fought and he walked out the door and didn't come back. "I don't know if I can watch you leave twice. I don't think I can do it."

"Then I won't leave," he says. "I'll stay with you as long as you want."

"No." I pull the blanket tighter. "It's just postponing the inevitable. Us lying here in bed together. It's almost unbearable."

"Yeah."

"Oliver. I'm going to do something very immature."

"Okay . . ."

"But it's all I know how to do right now."

"Okay," he repeats, his gaze so tender it hurts.

I pull the blanket over my head so I can't see him. "You can go now," I say from under the blanket. "Okay?"

I listen closely as the floorboards creak beneath his feet. I feel the warmth of his body as he leans in close and kisses the top of my head through the blanket. Then I hear the too-familiar sound of him walking out and shutting the bedroom door between us, for the second time.

Chapter Three

—

"**S**o he just left?" L'Wren shouts from the baseline.

I return her hit, hard. Too hard for a leisurely morning game of tennis. "He left. We both decided it was for the best."

L'Wren watches the ball whiz past, not bothering to run for it. "I'm sorry—but, Oliver, you do not get to just come over and have break-up sex with someone you've dressed up as Paw Patrol with for Halloween!"

"I invited him. And we didn't have sex."

"Please don't say 'just the tip.'"

"L'Wren! No. Please," I say, even though that's exactly what we did.

"Fine. *Almost sex,* whatever you want to call it." She pulls a new ball from the hem of her tennis skort and lifts her racket to serve.

"Can we actually stop here?" I call out. "I need time to shower before work."

"Oh thank god." She doubles over, dramatically clutching her knees. "I thought you'd make me play another set while we worked out all your Oliver demons. I'm dying over here."

We're both drenched in sweat. We tried to play early to beat the heat, but it's already 91 degrees at seven A.M. "Buy you an iced tea before you go?"

"You know what?" L'Wren has been giving me a steady stream of marital advice since we stepped out of the showers. The country club she and Kevin have recently joined is over-the-top, with thick, plush towels and cozy robes. L'Wren showed me the special chute you send your sweaty clothes down to be laundered, then we sampled every complimentary product on the well-lit vanities and used the high-speed hair dryers. At the club's bar, a silver-haired bartender refills our iced teas. "Let him live in that crappy loft . . ."

"It's not actually that bad. You saw it. And Emmy loves the pool—"

"Whatever," she dismisses. "Let him puff up and get bloaty on those sad, sodium-filled frozen dinners—"

"He looks great, L'Wren. He's training for a marathon. His whole body is getting . . ." I punch my fist into my palm like it's a brick wall.

"Fine." She rolls her eyes. "But think of what it feels like to be in a new space with all that *quiet*. . . . Dammit. This approach is not working. Now I want Oliver's life. . . . Okay, well, screw him for bettering himself after you break up. What a cliché! A total cliché, and it'll all come crashing down."

I laugh, poking at the perfectly crushed ice with my glass straw. "I just want . . ." I search for the right words at the bottom of my tea. "I wish I knew better what I wanted. When Oliver and I were together, I thought of him as so needy all the time. I used to picture him like an octopus with tentacles that were always reaching out for me, and it felt so suffocating. And now that he doesn't need me like that . . . Jesus, L'Wren, *I'm* the cliché."

"No, no. He's just not doing the things that turned you off anymore—or you're just not around to see them, so of course you're going to find him attractive again. It's confusing."

"It's sad. I know, *of course* it's sad, we're separated. But I guess I wasn't expecting to be *this sad* and this lost. It doesn't feel over. That's the part I can't figure out. After we had Emmy, I knew we were done having kids. I knew it in my bones. Our family was complete. But this separation . . . It feels like purgatory. Like we're just ghosts haunting each other. Is there something still there? Am I just wearing my rose-tinted glasses?"

When I lift my head, L'Wren takes me firmly by both shoulders. "Follow the white light, Diana. It's time."

I smile. "I know. You're right. We're light-years away from each other. The other night proved that."

"Great." She claps her hands together decisively, but her smile is full of affection. "We're moving forward and you are *not* alone. New topic. What else?"

A perfect opening. A chance to tell her all about Dirty Diana and my hope that it will become a real thing. But how do I tell her? And what is it? Me listening to other people's fantasies in the middle of the night? Trying to make it into a project to stave off loneliness? When the house is too quiet, I put on headphones and try to hear something in these stories about desire, other people's fantasies for the future, something lifting them up out of clichés about power-swapping and lust and into . . . ? What am I looking for? I feel useless and lost.

L'Wren's phone vibrates on the bar beside us. When she checks the text, she breaks into a massive grin.

"Who's that?"

She sets the phone down again, this time screen face down. "Hmm?"

"You have this big smile. What's so funny?"

L'Wren waves a hand to tell me it's nothing. "Arthur. The vet who's helping me out with the cat rescue. I told you about him."

I shake my head.

"No? I haven't? Oh yeah, he's helping me with a crazy influx of foster kittens, thank god. He *loves* cats."

"I would hope so." After years of taking in stray cats, L'Wren has started her own rescue.

She lifts her phone and shows me the text. It's a picture of a cat wearing a lemon wedge on his head like a hat.

"Is this cat humor?"

"So bizarre, right?" She rolls her eyes. "He loves cats."

"I got that."

She gives a hollow laugh but doesn't meet my eyes. "He's obsessed. Weird, right?" The only weird thing is L'Wren calling another cat person weird.

"He sounds perfect for the job."

"Did I tell you he works out with them? Look at this!"

She pulls up another photo, this one of a guy's chest, close up and shirtless, doing bicep curls with two cats.

"Why's his face cut off?"

She snatches the phone back. "Because it's about the *cats,* Diana. I mean, if you're into that. Look at those tabby girls! Sweet sisters."

I peek one more time at the arms and chest that take up most of the frame. "This is like a cat lady's dick pic, L'Wren."

"Diana! Stop. Arthur is a doctor."

"And?"

She slips her phone into her purse.

"L'Wren. Do you have a little crush on the vet?"

"No! What? No!" I try to remember the last time I saw L'Wren blush. "We work together. And I'm married. And he's just fun. Fun to talk to."

A comforting sensation washes over me. I'm not the only one of us who's keeping secrets.

I left my sunglasses at the club but only realize once I'm nearly at work and it's too late to turn back. I drive east, squinting into the sun. The rays splinter my vision, reminding me of a glaringly white, blank canvas. I imagine how I'd fill it right now if I could. I'd use oil paints in dark colors and thick strokes to fill the entire space, like a night sky. I am spending far too much time thinking about Oliver. Jasper, I allow myself to think about because he is so far away.

At work, I walk past Oliver's nearly empty office. There's still a framed school picture of Emmy with two missing front teeth and his UT diploma collecting dust on the wall.

"It's weird," our receptionist, Talia, says as she passes me in the hall, "I keep expecting him to be there too." I feel my cheeks burn. I smile and grab my mail from her. "Oh, and Diana? Allen wants to see you. ASAP."

The sentence fills me with dread. My father-in-law runs a wealth management firm, where I've worked for the past fifteen years. We help clients with their investments and possessions, making my father-in-law richer in the process. Typically, Allen likes to be involved in each and every piece of advice we give a client—from tax planning to real estate, down to which model car they should buy—but ever since Oliver and I separated, Allen and I have been good at steering clear of each other.

There is no putting it off this morning. I head directly for Allen's office and knock on his open door. He looks up, his eyes bright and his hair combed perfectly. His office smells like aftershave and leather. When I'm in here, I imagine a cow wearing cologne. "Hi, sweetheart. Come on in."

"Everything okay?"

"I should be asking you that."

"I'm good. Fine. We're all okay."

"I hate it." He bangs his fist, lightly but dramatically, against his desk. "This separation. Vivian and I just hate it." We both know my mother-in-law doesn't hate it. "It's hard for everyone, but you're still my daughter-in-law. The mother of my Number One Grandbaby. I don't need a piece of paper to tell me that." He gives me his sympathy smile—I know it well. It's exactly like Oliver's, the way their mouths turn up slightly more on the right than the left. Their happy smiles are even and full.

"Thank you." His hands, too, now folded on the desk in front of him, are so much like Oliver's.

"So, Casino Royale. See you there?"

"Sorry?"

"That's Viv's theme this year. She's flying in real Vegas dealers or some crap, should be a hell of a good time." Once a year, my mother-in-law throws a party for the firm's top executives, switching up the theme every time. Denim and Diamonds. Boots and Bow Ties. Always extravagant and over-the-top. "We invited Oliver but he RSVP'd no. God only knows what that boy's up to."

"Allen, this is very kind, but you don't have to include me—"

"Petra Rowling has just RSVP'd yes. It's a perfect opportunity to make an introduction."

"Oh." Petra is the recent widow of one of Allen's biggest clients, footballer Mitch Martin, who died tragically in a private plane crash earlier this year. Mitch played for the Cowboys, and he and Petra were married young. When he retired, they filmed their own reality show, which became insanely popular for its unfiltered peek into their marriage. Petra now has a cookbook line. Multiple sponsorships. All of it.

"I'd love it if you could come by and say hello, spend a little time with Petra at the party, make sure she has fun. I want her to feel good about Mitch's money staying with the firm."

"Oh." It clicks into place. Allen needs a woman to talk to Petra, to prove that one actually works at the firm, and I'm his only choice. "Isn't it her money too?"

"Of course, yes, and this is all in Petra's best interest. I worry about all the vultures knocking on her door. I thought it would be nice for her to have some of your . . . *energy* at the party."

My in-laws' historic Tudor glows from within. It might be from the thousands of tea lights Vivian's staff has carefully set up throughout. There must be twenty servers in crisp white shirts and black aprons standing at attention in the foyer like toy soldiers. One of them hands me a glass of champagne and I fight the urge to take two. Vivian rushes to greet me and is oddly warm, which is way more unnerving than her iciness.

"You look beautiful, Diana. Thank you so much for coming. I know it's not easy to be here."

"You've outdone yourself again," I say, as she gives me a quick, tight hug.

"It all comes together in the end, doesn't it?" Vivian smiles, and I smile, too, and I realize we've already run out of things to say to each other. I'm relieved when Allen swans in and leads me straight to Petra.

"There she is!" Allen announces, his voice booming through the backyard, where someone has stretched an enormous canvas, painted to look like Monaco's coastline, lit from below with giant spotlights. It's gaudy and bright and Petra is smart to have found the darkest corner, at a small table near the bar.

Petra is stunning. Her dark hair is parted down the middle and tucked into a low bun, one wavy strand framing her face. Her dress is emerald-colored silk and floor-length. It's early in the night, but she's already barefoot, her red-bottomed stilettos resting on the table in front of her.

"Petra," Allen booms again. "How are you?"

"It's a lovely party, Allen." Petra smiles warmly, then turns to me. "You must be Diana."

"It's so nice to meet you." I've never met someone in person whom I've seen on TV. I feel awkward and stiff, like I should have more to say. In preparation for tonight, I watched an entire season of Petra's reality show and I know all kinds of intimate details about her. I know that her mother is Scottish and her father is Nigerian and that she grew up in London and was kicked out of two boarding schools before graduating from a third with honors. She met her husband at a rugby match in Wales where they were both guests of the club's owner, and it was love at first sight. "You must hear this all the time, but I feel like I know you already."

"Say that again . . ."

"Sorry?"

"Say it again."

"Which part?"

"Any of it." Petra studies my face. "Your voice sounds *so* familiar."

"Does it?" I feel the tips of my ears go pink. There's no way she's heard my Dirty Diana interviews, is there? How many people has Alicia sent them to?

"Where do I know it from? This is going to drive me crazy."

"Diana's voice?" Allen pipes in. "No, you wouldn't know it. She hasn't answered the front desk phone in years. She's worked her way right up the ladder, as we like to see happen at the firm—and now, invaluable. A great fit."

It's really a gift he has—managing to make all three of us feel uncomfortable in so few words. "Well." He claps his hands together. "I'll leave you two to get acquainted. Don't miss the carving station. Vivian had the prime rib prepared by Chef Dennis." Allen winks, then disappears.

Petra immediately stage-whispers, "Who the fuck is Chef Dennis and how long before I can make an Irish exit?"

I laugh harder than I should. "I'm asking myself the same question." Then, because not to feels like too big a betrayal of my in-laws, I offer, "I can make us a plate in the meantime?"

"You're sweet. I'm a vegetarian. Should I admit that in this crowd?" She narrows her eyes and scans the room.

"Are you also sober and an atheist?" I slip into the seat across from her. "Because my mother-in-law will have you escorted out."

"Ohhh," she breathes, a twinkle in her eye. "Allen is your boss *and* your father-in-law."

"Yes. Sort of."

I can see from the way her brow crinkles that she caught the "sort of," but she doesn't push. Just over Petra's shoulder, I notice Vivian's oldest friend, Joy, breaking away from her group of melting socialites and heading directly for us. Before I can find a corner to cower in, she's at my side, dressed in head-to-toe Carolina Herrera.

"Diana. *Honey.* Vivian told me about you and Oliver. I'm in shock. Absolute shock. You two were so darling together."

"Thank you." I see her hands clutch her heart and want to roll my eyes. "Joy, this is my friend Petra."

Joy smiles tightly at Petra and returns her focus to me. "I remember your wedding day like it was yesterday. Well, you proved everyone wrong for a while there, didn't you? You lasted a good long while."

"We did. Yes."

"Vivian is just shattered, as you know. We can't handle this kind of stress at our age. Stress is the silent killer, and I don't need any more than I already have. I cried all day. The entire day. I couldn't get out of the bed when Vivian told me. And poor sweet Emmy. I cry for her as well. I really do."

"Diana!" Petra scolds, leaning across the table, reaching for my elbow. "Did you have any idea your divorce was causing Joy so much distress?"

I press my lips together and try not to smile. "I did not." I crane my neck to look up at Joy. "I'm terribly sorry."

"I'll save you the gory details of the end of my marriage, Joy," Petra interjects. "He died. Suddenly. Private plane. *Very* stressful."

"Oh dear." Joy's face contorts in horror.

"In fact, Diana, I don't think it's fair for us to be at this party with our depressing backstories. We don't want to cause the guests any undue trouble. You know what, darling? I think this might be our cue."

To Joy's total confusion, Petra grabs my hand and her shoes and we slip through the party and out the front door. It feels like committing a delicious, giddy crime. Petra runs toward her driver, who holds open the door of a ridiculously large black car, the size of a small home. It has deep, plush seats and a privacy partition separating the back from the front.

As we climb in, Petra asks, "Do I smell like death?"

For a moment I freeze—I think of her husband and whether there's something appropriate I'm supposed to say.

"From all those fucking meat stations." She wrinkles her nose.

"Oh." I laugh. "No. Maybe. A little?"

"Smell my dress." She leans into me, the nape of her neck brushing against my cheek.

"No, you smell like . . . tea rose?"

"Mitch's favorite," she says matter-of-factly, settling into the bench seat next to me and stretching out her legs. She looks tiny in this big car.

"I'm so sorry for your loss," I say.

She turns to me and grins. "Is it stressing you out? Have you been in bed all day?"

I take her cue. "It's a lot for me, yes."

"Of course. Totally understandable. I'll send both you and Joy a fruit basket."

I laugh, and when the car falls quiet, I say, "I really am sorry. It's very unfair."

"Thank you." She squeezes my knee, as if to tell me she's okay. "He was one of the good ones. And he liked Allen very much. But I'm afraid if you've been sent to convince me to keep our money at the firm, I have to tell you don't bother. I haven't decided what to do yet, and I won't be convinced just because someone nice with a vagina works at the firm. No offense. Honestly, I find you better than nice already."

She doesn't wait for a response but opens the car's fridge compartment and takes out a clear glass bottle with some sort of fizzy amber liquid inside. She pours it into a glass for me, then dips back into the fridge for another bottle, this time the liquid a cloudy purple, and pours herself a glass.

"Allen can be . . ." I start. "He means well."

Petra drops ice into each of our glasses. "Mitch always liked being told what to do by rich old dudes. It was his one flaw. And he had a soft spot for Allen. I never totally got it."

"Allen is trustworthy."

"Maybe. And Mitch liked to win. Allen always looks like he's winning. He looks like *generations of winning*. Cheers."

We clink glasses and I take a sip. "Mmm." I'm surprised by how something on ice can taste so warm. And also musty. Like an old wool scarf stored over a long, hot summer. "It's different. Frothy."

"Homemade kombucha. Do you like it?"

"No." I shake my head and we both laugh. "It's terrible."

"But so amazing for the gut. Here. Try mine." She hands me her glass. "Maybe it's the passion fruit in yours that you don't like."

It feels intimate, drinking from her glass. I take a sip. "Mmm." I cough.

"It's not that bad!"

"Mmm," I repeat and we both laugh.

"You're funny." It's what someone says when they're surprised you have a personality. I should be insulted but I'm thrilled. I'm consumed by the feeling of wanting Petra to like me.

"So . . ." She sits back in her seat. "You and your husband are separated?" Petra takes in every part of my face—my eyes, my nose, my lips. "But you still work at the firm? For Allen?"

"For now. Not forever. I don't think. Oliver, my—ex?—he's still between jobs. So it's good for one of us to be working."

Petra opens her car door, then grabs my glass, abruptly emptying it onto Vivian and Allen's driveway. She opens the car's fridge again, this time mixing me a gin and tonic, then pours a generous amount of gin into her own glass.

"You know," she tells me, "Mitch didn't create our brand. I did. If he hadn't met me, he would have played a few more years of pro football and gone back to Odessa and bought all his friends McMansions and Lambos. He'd have run out of money in less than two years.

"I introduced him to couture and, when the time was right, bought him his first set of veneers and prepped him before every interview. My husband was lovely, but he was never all that ambitious. I was. The show, the brand partnerships, even the Nike commercial, were all my concepts. We turned 'honesty' into our brand . . ." Her voice trails off, as if she's suddenly grown tired of reading her own press release.

"I'm sure you miss him very much."

"And as for the money . . ." She picks up a thread neither of us had started, then stops. Her fingers tap against her glass, then hover gently against her lips, then return to her glass. After a long pause she begins again, somewhere else. "Some days I wake up and I know exactly where I'm going. And others, I can't let my feet touch the floor. I open my eyes and feel so lost that I'm afraid if I sit up in bed the whole room will spin or fade away. So I stay really still. Like maybe if I don't move, I won't feel so lost. As if it's me who's been mislaid."

From outside, I hear the faraway noises of party laughter and Vivian's hired band. Inside the car, it's only the sound of Petra and me breathing and, faintly, through the driver's partition, the muffled echoes of a baseball game on the radio: the crack of the bat and an announcer's excited call. I know I should eventually bring up Allen again and all the reasons the firm is actually the *perfect fit,* but it feels so tedious.

A swath of light from Vivian's casino lights washes across Petra's bare shoulder, the hand holding her glass, her profile. When she turns to look at me, her entire face moves into shadow. "I get why you still work there."

"Yeah?" Maybe she could help me understand.

"It's safe and contained. I could use more of that. I'm a little jealous."

"I have other interests, apart from the firm." Without hesitation, I tell her all about Dirty Diana. I don't know why I start talking, but Petra seems so open, so honest and real and not at all judgy, and once I begin, it all spills out. She doesn't take her eyes off me, and holding her attention is intoxicating. I tell her about how I haven't been sleeping since Oliver moved out, about how restless I've been and how when I lie awake recently, I think about getting on a plane and going anywhere. I don't mention Jasper, but I do say maybe Europe? London, or maybe Paris, to be inspired. The more I talk, the easier it is to tell her things. Things I've been burning to tell L'Wren but haven't. When I come up for air, I feel like I'm floating.

Petra holds out her palm. "Let me see your phone." I unlock it and hand it over so she can add her details. "I leave for Europe in a week. Mitch and I always spent our summers there. I'll be in Paris all of June, part of July. Then maybe Greece? Switzerland maybe? Don't know. Call me when you get there."

Chapter Four

—

May slips into June and the last weeks of school push what was once a manageable but packed schedule into something more chaotic. I am so consumed with keeping the details and schedules straight—end-of-year parties, performances, soccer games, shuttling Emmy from Oliver's house to my own—that I manage to make it so that I can't think much more than a day ahead. Except for making summer plans for Emmy. After many back-and-forth texts with Oliver, we've agreed to let her go to sleepaway camp with Halston for a week, like she's been begging to do.

But she's so little, I insisted.

Oliver texted back pictures of happy kids in canoes and reminded me, *I went there every summer for eleven years. And look at me!*

. . . Exactly.

Ha ha. Too soon.

What if she doesn't like it?

Her best friend and s'mores? She'll be fine.

Then he texted me a long speech about independence and confidence that I think he cut and pasted from the camp's website.

Okay, I finally agreed because I knew how badly Emmy wanted to go and the only thing in the way was how much I was going to miss her.

I follow the camp packing list to a T, buying her an extra bathing suit and labeling every piece of clothing going in her camp duffel. And today on my lunch break, with two days left in the school year, I race home to grab the watermelon slices that need to be dropped off at the school picnic by 12:15, sharp.

Running out the door, I spot Emmy's ballet bag. I hurry to the car and dial Oliver. "Hey, it's me. I forgot to give you Emmy's ballet clothes for class this afternoon. I can leave them on your mat on my way to drop off fruit that needs to be at her school in the next thirty minutes or the world starts to fall in on itself." I fake laugh at my own dumb joke, a weird fake laugh that I've heard myself using with him more and more since the night we almost slept together. It makes me cringe every time. Since that night, Oliver and I have kept our conversations focused on Emmy. Like we'd become so good at doing over the last few years, we avoid an uncomfortable conversation and pretend the evening didn't happen, silently agreeing to slip it under the rug with the rest of our issues.

At his building, I pass two gorgeous women in barely there bikinis soaking in the sun by the pool. Is this who Oliver asks to borrow milk from when he runs out? I drop Emmy's pink ballet bag on his doorstep and as soon as I turn to go, his door opens. "Diana?"

"You're home?"

"Yeah. I'm just making coffee. You want some?"

"I called from the car. I thought maybe you were at an interview."

"Want to come in?"

I take in his bare feet, his cutoff shorts, and a T-shirt worn so thin the collar is frayed. He looks handsome, well-rested, and tan, like he's on vacation instead of standing in his own doorway on a Tuesday. "Come on inside."

In his living room hangs a giant charcoal drawing of a bear. When did Oliver start buying art? "Where did you get . . ."

"I don't have an interview today."

"Oh. They've already hired someone?"

"No, no, they want to meet but . . ." He shrugs. "I don't want it. It's more of the same, I realized. Different office, different people, same shit." He sounds like a broody artist on the verge of a creative breakthrough. Maybe *he* drew the charcoal bear. Maybe I shouldn't pretend to be able to guess what he's thinking anymore.

I follow him to the kitchen, where he grinds beans for our coffee and says loudly over the noise, "I actually haven't been going on any of the interviews. I've been lying about that."

"You haven't been going on job interviews?" The grating noise stops. "Since you walked out on your job? Not a single one?"

"Nope." He smiles. "But hang on, I do know what I'm doing. In fact, I've never been happier. Maybe you should quit that place too."

My face prickles with heat as I watch him froth milk for my coffee. After several long minutes of watching him make an elaborate coffee while wondering how pissed I should be, he hands me a full white mug with a photo screened onto it. A picture of Oliver and Emmy at some kind of carnival I wasn't invited to or even ever heard about. "Okay. So what *are* you doing? Borrowing money from your dad?"

It's a low blow, but instead of getting defensive, he laughs a strange "as if" guffaw, and I think but do not say, *What the fuck, Oliver, how is that funny?* As if *we haven't ever borrowed money from them before,* as if *they didn't help us with the down payment on our house years ago.*

He picks up a printout from the kitchen table and hands it to me. It's an MLS listing for a small Tudor home not far from here. Built in 1927, the description reads, it's only had three owners and retains most of the original details. It's charming, like something out of a fairy tale—large windows with diamond-shaped panes and a round front door like a small castle.

"I'm flipping it. It doesn't need much. New paint, new kitchen, and baths. Tear up the carpet and pray for hardwood floors kind of thing. But the wall paneling and ceiling beams are all original."

"Flipping it? With who?"

"I bought it out of probate for dirt cheap and I'm doing most of it myself. I picked up my tools from my parents' garage. Remember that old sawhorse? I was sure my mom had thrown it out. And the power washer. She kept her word and held on to all of it. It feels so good to get back to work. With the help of a few YouTube videos."

"YouTube videos?"

He smiles and takes the flier from my hands. "Diana? Why are you only responding in questions?"

"Because I am catching up, Oliver." I let out a long, slow exhale. "Or trying to. How did you pay for this house?"

"Deep breath, Diana. I'm going to put it all back."

"No . . ." The blood drains from my face. "From our account?"

"Yes, *ours*. And I only touched my half, which I'm going to double. Just give me six months."

My half? We haven't even halved yet. Have we?

"I'm so confused, Oliver. You didn't think to ask me first?"

"Diana, our assets are on their way to being divided anyway. Right?"

The color rushes back to my face. I blush with the shame of my avoidance. But I'm not the only one who has been avoiding talking about our separation. So why does it all look so carefree on him?

"It's going to work," he says. "Turns out, I'm really good at this."

His relaxed lean against his kitchen counter in his bare feet and his stupid fucking shorts are making my blood boil. I'm sweating in a beige suit on my forty-five-minute lunch hour.

"How do you know?" I snap. "Anyone can watch a YouTube video."

"Ouch."

"You don't think I should be pissed? We have one paycheck right now. Mine. And then you tell me to quit my job when it's the only job we have?"

"Because maybe there's something out there that might make you happier. I was really confused, Diana. For so long. Doing what everyone around me wanted me to do. But I finally found something I love."

The hair on my arms raises in a kind of cold fury. "How nice."

"I thought you would be happy for me."

"When were you going to tell me all this? If I hadn't come over today?"

"Okay, but I am telling you now. And I would have—"

I want to scream, but instead my voice comes out like a hiss. "Is this some kind of HGTV midlife crisis?"

Oliver rakes his hands through his hair the way he does when he's trying not to get frustrated. "I get that you're pissed. But, Diana, of the two of us, you have to admit, I've always been the one who managed the finances. When we met, you were broke—"

"I think you should stop talking."

"Diana, c'mon, it's not like I'm not really good with money."

"Because you were fucking *born into it*—" My rage is coming so fast and thick, the words get stuck in my throat. "No." I shake my head. "Not right now. I'm late. To drop off fucking watermelon." I immediately regret adding the watermelon detail. It sounded more potent in my head.

My rant is followed by a very nondramatic exit. Instead of slamming the door, I put my mug of frustratingly good coffee in his sink, and then Oliver holds the door open for me. He quietly follows me to my car.

Neither of us says a word until I'm sitting in the driver's seat. My car is hot and smells like rotting fruit. "I have to go to work," I tell him, placing an emphasis on "work."

He leans against the open window. "Please come and see the house. If you could see what I do, you might change your mind."

That afternoon, I'm back at my desk for less than thirty minutes when Allen sticks his head in. "Petra just called. You two must have really hit it off." His smile is somewhere between his sympathy half smile and a genuinely happy grin. "She wants to meet with you in Paris and discuss her relationship with our firm."

"Petra?"

"Those were her words. She said since you were meaning to make the trip to Paris anyway . . ."

"Oh, I mentioned maybe going—" I hadn't left the country since Emmy was born. Oliver and I had made plans to travel to Europe, but they were always postponed by work or the cost of a new hot water heater or needing a new roof. The idea of getting on a plane and landing in Paris makes me want to tackle Allen in a bear hug.

"Right. Of course." Allen winks, picking up on my excitement. "You should go. Petra needs to make someone jump through a few hoops for her and she's chosen you."

"Okay, that's great. Thank you." I don't know whether to be grateful to Petra or unnerved that she's interfering in my life. I choose grateful.

When Allen lingers in the doorway, I ask him if everything is all right.

"Sure." He lowers his voice. "Things at the firm this year . . . It would be helpful to us. To me. If you could get this done with Petra." Since we'd met, Allen has never shown any kind of vulnerability in front of me. He's never asked for my help once. Standing in my office doorway, he looks ten years older.

"Yes. Of course."

"Terrific." He perks right back up. "I'll have Cindy help with flights. And we've already prepared some decks to review before you leave."

The next day, on my lunch break, Liam meets me at the mall and is quickly crestfallen when we beeline for the luggage store. "Who shops on an empty stomach?"

"I do."

He sighs and trails me into the store. It's clean and brightly lit, suitcases lined neatly against every wall. Liam is L'Wren's stepson and like a little brother to me. I still haven't told L'Wren about Liam helping me with Dirty Diana. He's the only one in Rockgate whom I've told about Dirty Diana, and when Alicia and I needed extra help figuring out how to build a website, he was the perfect, least judgmental person to turn to. When I'd first asked him, he beamed. "I get it, *entrepreneur to entrepreneur.*" He'd gestured around the basement (L'Wren's basement, which he was old enough to move out of years ago) to the piles of bloody prosthetics and special effects he creates and sells online. "You need to scale the ambition, and there's only so far you can push that boulder up the hill on your own. Right?" Liam is creative and messy, and since the day we met each of us has had an overwhelming desire to bail the other out.

"Can I assist you?" A man with an Italian accent, wearing an impeccably fitted gray flannel suit, appears before us and introduces himself as Enzo.

"She's looking for a suitcase . . ." Liam helps me out.

"Of course, do we know what size?"

"Something I can carry on."

"For international travel. She's going to Paris."

"Oh, *magnifique.*" Enzo smiles. His hair is thick and dark and his eyes a deep brown. He rattles off details about the luggage all around us and Liam nods along. Enzo pulls out different models, and I try not to get too distracted by the way his elegant fingers clasp and unclasp each one.

He asks me about my trip and I tell him I'm going there for work. He nods and says, "and some fun," then writes down the name of his favorite cafés and a bar that his best friend from grade school runs. I tell him I'll definitely check it out. For a moment I get lost, picturing sitting at a Parisian bar next to Enzo.

"Diana? Sage or terra-cotta?" Liam is asking.

"It's perfect."

They both laugh, asking "Which one?," and my cheeks burn.

"Sage."

"She'll take it."

"Wonderful! Let me get us a brand-new one from the back." When he turns, Liam raises his eyebrows and smiles. I roll my eyes. But I'm caught.

"Give him your number," Liam whispers, and I dig my elbow into his ribs to shut him up. "What?" he says innocently. "He clearly likes to travel. He's *Italian*."

Enzo reappears. "Here we are."

"Diana loves to travel."

I shoot Liam a look.

"Oh yeah?"

"Do you travel a lot?" Liam asks him, and I blush a deeper shade of pink.

"Every chance I get," Enzo says. "A perk of being single."

Liam beams like *bingo* and I dig for my wallet.

In line for pretzels, Liam sighs. "God. That was embarrassing. You need to freshen up on your flirting."

"I wasn't flirting."

"I know, I was being generous with my word choice. I don't know what to call that awkward dance back there."

"Shut up." I laugh.

We sit at a sticky table and I try not to imagine which corner of the food court it was that Oliver and the pixie-haired lady first met.

"Want some?" Liam tears off a piece of his cinnamon sugar pretzel and offers it to me.

"Liam. Entrepreneur to entrepreneur"—I see his eyes twinkle—"do you still think it's possible to slowly build out Dirty Diana ourselves?"

Liam and I are both aware of our roles—that I'm the finance person and he's the one with cinnamon sugar on his chin—but he's also full of creative ideas and he knows that right now I'm not really looking for an answer, only a bit of support, the kind of good-natured encouragement that he gives wholeheartedly.

"I'm way ahead of you. Yes. And you're going to love my new layouts. I modeled one with a monthly subscription in mind. But. You're going to need more content." He takes another bite, then finishes off his lemonade. "I get it. Why you're going to Paris."

"I'm going to Paris for work."

He smirks. "Sure. Okay then, I get why you're asking about expanding the site."

"Oh yeah?"

"Yeah."

"And?"

"You should have something of your own. Sure, to possibly make some cash. But mostly so your soul doesn't shrivel up and die on the baking-hot suburban sidewalks of Rockgate like the souls of so many women in lululemon leggings before you."

I try not to smile too big as I help myself to Liam's pretzel, ripping off a generous piece. The hum of the lunchtime crowd fills the silence for us, until finally I say, "It really is a work trip. Allen's paying." I take a bite and think of calling Jasper while I'm there.

Liam tips back in his chair, seeming to read my every thought. "Yeah, for work."

. . .

On my way home that evening, I call Alicia from the car. Alicia and I talk most mornings but today we missed each other. We've been friends since our twenties and lately she is also the driving force behind me making something—anything—out of the Dirty Diana interviews, as we've come to think of them. I think she wants me to get lost in something creative right now, especially so I don't brood over Oliver.

"Paris! Paris, France?"

"It would be easier if it was Paris, Texas."

"Do you need an assistant?"

"For what?"

"Literally anything. I'll wash your delicates in the sink. I'll drive you around town. I'll edit every single Parisian fantasy. I'll give you my fantasy! Just take me!"

"This is a work trip. Alicia? I hear you typing. Are you buying a ticket as we speak?"

"Diana. I literally found a cheddar goldfish under my boob this morning. I think I need to get away. We can make it a Dirty Diana work trip."

"Not Dirty Diana. I'm meeting a client."

"Got it. Dirty Diana is still the side hustle. Oh . . . cheap flights out of Dallas."

"This Sunday?" L'Wren steals a glance at me from the driver's seat as we carpool home from a school meeting.

"It's a work trip, L'Wren." There is something in "work trip" no one wants to hear.

"Exactly. You're meeting with *one* important client, right? Is that going to take five days? Two dinners at the most. Then what will you do? I know Paris like the back of my hand." She speaks quickly, hardly taking a breath. "It's *perfect* timing. Halston and Emmy can have a sleepover at Oliver's on Sunday and then he can drop them at camp on Monday. He wouldn't mind, would he? Probably better than us dropping them and getting emotional just watching them go."

She's only been to Paris twice, but compared to me, she does know it like the back of her hand. "An old friend from Santa Fe is coming with me."

"Alicia?"

"Yes." I worry the news will hurt L'Wren's feelings, that I've invited someone else.

But she smiles brightly and says, "Can't wait to meet her. You know I get along with everyone." This is not true, but I love that L'Wren thinks it. "We'll have a great time."

"It's a work trip." I throw it out one more time, for my own amusement now.

"Of course. But I need out of Dallas for a minute. Not like, oh fun, Paris, can I come? It's more than that."

Her voice hitches.

"L'Wren . . ."

Her eyes well with tears and she pulls off the frontage road and turns the engine off in a 7-Eleven parking lot. "If I don't go to Paris with you, I might sleep with Arthur. Multiple times."

"Oh, L'Wren."

"I can't even think about it, but it's also all I think about. How is this possible? I wish I'd never met him."

I undo my seatbelt and rest my hand on hers. "Are you and Kevin in a bad spot?"

"It's the same. He's the same. He doesn't notice how distracted I am. What does that mean?"

"Kevin has always been a bit distracted himself. With work, I mean."

"Well, I need a Parisian distraction now." She wipes her eyes and prepares to get back on the highway. "I'll put us up in the very best hotel. We'll have some girl time. I could really use it, Diana. You'd be doing me a favor."

L'Wren had been doing me favors since she took me under her wing back when Emmy was in pre-K. She told me where to enroll Emmy in school, she got me into all the best after-school activities, and she advised me which parents to avoid in the carpool lane. I would have been lost without her.

"Sure. The more the merrier."

When L'Wren drops me at home, I'm glad there isn't a single light on, so the house can just suck me into its darkness and I can hide in here awhile. I feel my way down the hall, my hand gliding along the walls all the way up the stairs to my bedroom. I lie on the bed and think about all the things I should do—edit new interviews and finish a painting, fold the laundry, sign up for Emmy's soccer season, pay that one online bill that never charges my credit card on file.

In the bathroom, I strip off my clothes and shower in the dark. I slip into bed and search for old streaming episodes of Petra's show and spend the next three hours watching her and Mitch. They sign up for a cooking class and learn how to make waffles. In the next episode, she teaches him how to drive stick. In between antics, they agree they don't want children and lie in bed talking about what the future might look like: She wants to go to Cuba, he wants to try fly-fishing. The sound of their light disagreements lulls me to sleep.

PART TWO

Paris

Chapter Five

———

Alicia is standing in front of the Yogurtland at Dallas Fort Worth International Airport, wearing a lavender beret. *"Bonjour!"* she cries. She hands L'Wren a matching red beret, felt and limp. "So nice to meet you, L'Wren," she says, hugging her. L'Wren looks less than pleased. For me Alicia pulls out a cream-colored baseball cap with *Paris* written inside a shamrock of green sequins. "It was the tackiest I could find." I put it on and admire myself in a strip of mirror outside the duty-free store.

We reach our gate with time to spare. Alicia unzips her roller bag to show us how meticulously she has packed, squashing everything into small cubes and three-ounce containers. There was a whole year in her twenties, I remember, when Alicia didn't even use a wallet, just carried around a plastic Walgreen's bag and stashed her credit cards and any cash she had inside.

Once we board, I settle into my first-class seat, in its own pod, fully reclinable, with a feather duvet, two pillows, and a toiletry bag of fancy samples. L'Wren is directly behind me, slipping off her shoes. I poke my head down the aisle, trying to spot Alicia.

"I'm sorry," L'Wren says, catching my frown. "Upgrading you was supposed to be a good surprise."

"No. It's amazing. Way too generous. I just feel a little bad for Alicia."

"She was always going to fly coach, wasn't she? Nothing has changed for her."

"Yes, but I was also going to fly coach. We were going to sit next to each other."

"She's not twelve, Diana. She's fine."

"Of course."

But once the plane is in the air and the first round of drinks is served, I slip out of my seat and past L'Wren, already deep in a Xanax sleep. I carry my chilled glass of champagne and make my way to Alicia. It's worse than I feared—a middle seat between a panicked-looking man with a baby and a much older man who is already snoring. Alicia is deep into reading her book and still wearing her beret.

When she spots me, I raise the glass—"Cheers! To Paris!"—and hand her the champagne.

Alicia grins. "You're embarrassing me in front of my new homies."

After a few minutes of our whispered chitchat, the snoring man lifts his sleep mask. "She's fine. Go back to first class."

We fly through the night. As I drift off to sleep, I imagine I'm flying to meet Jasper, who will pick me up at the airport with a bouquet of wildflowers and whisk me off to the south of France for a few delicious days in the sun. But after I change into my bikini in the villa bathroom, I open the doors and see Oliver waiting on the bed, in a bright blue swimsuit, his chest tanned, his eyes sparkling. I startle awake, disoriented. I try to distract myself with the TV. I scroll the screen forever and then finally decide on a *Seinfeld* rerun. It reminds me too much of watching TV with Oliver, though, so I shut it off. I look out the window and eventually drift off watching the red flash of taillights.

Halfway through the flight, I head back to Alicia, who is still engrossed in her book, looking tired. I convince her to swap seats with me. After some maneuvering, I manage to find a position on my side, my knees pulled to my chest, and drift into the very shallowest part of dozing. Then the cabin lights come up, too bright, and breakfast is served. While I pick at my croissant and sip my lukewarm orange juice, I think about texting Jasper. Should I let him know I'm coming to Europe? He was the one who initiated all this. What would happen if I told him I was in Paris?

L'Wren and I stand watch over her mountain of luggage while Alicia goes in search of a big enough taxi. L'Wren spritzes my face with something cool and rose-scented and hands me a pouch of powdered vitamin C. "For the jet lag." She raises her bottled water as if to make a toast. "Look at us. You have been through hell the last couple of months. I have been tempted for the first time in my life and have acid reflux my acupuncturist can't cure. We're going to leave that behind in Rockgate. We are new women. You're going to say yes to my suggestions, right?"

"Sure." I smile. "Within reason."

"No. With no reason. We are going to say yes to the most insane ideas no matter what they are. For five whole days."

"Okay."

"Not 'okay.'"

"*Yes.* Yes, L'Wren."

"Perfect. So here's the itinerary"—she pulls up a list on her phone—"with a few tiny little gaps for your meetings."

. . .

Once our luggage is neatly stacked in the trunk and along the front bench of the taxi, I cram myself between Alicia and L'Wren in the back seat. I feel dazzled, in awe even of the foreignness of the bland roads around the airport. We gaze quietly at the scenery until we near our hotel, the beauty of the city center unfolding before us.

"Even the dogs are chicer in Paris! Look at their fashionable little coats!" Alicia says.

"Did I show you Arthur's dog? I'm not even a dog person, but this dog is something else."

L'Wren pulls up a photo of a handsome white-and-black husky.

Alicia peers at L'Wren's phone. "Is Arthur your husband?"

"No! Oh no. Arthur works with me. He volunteers with my rescue."

I recognize a familiar posture in Alicia—she leans forward, curious. "Why do you have a picture of his dog on your phone?"

"L'Wren loves animals."

"I don't know why," L'Wren says flatly. "I guess because he's cute."

Alicia settles back in her seat and looks out the window as we idle in traffic. I'm relieved that she's lost interest. Then she says, "Does your husband like Arthur?" We're not even to the hotel yet, and my fears about the two of them clashing are coming true.

"My husband?" L'Wren says lightly. "Mmm. Kevin doesn't like anyone really."

"How is he doing? I mean . . . I really like Kevin." I feel both women looking at me so I stare straight ahead, at the back of the driver's cap, then fake a yawn.

"I'm so glad to know you like him, Diana." L'Wren laughs. "He's in London actually. Some high-stakes something or other."

"Are you going to see him?" Alicia isn't dropping it.

"I hadn't planned on it."

"He's so close. A romantic night in Paris?"

"Are *you* going to see your husband?" L'Wren returns fire.

"My husband is in Santa Fe."

"I'm just grateful I don't have a husband!" I blurt. "We all have nice husbands except me and nice kids and lovely people with dogs that we like in our lives. Oh look! The Eiffel Tower."

"This is a perfect light." Alicia turns for a better view. "We need a picture!"

I look at L'Wren. I sense the last thing she wants to do is stop, but she smiles and says, "It is the trip of *yes.*"

As we pull up to the hotel, L'Wren explains that during one of the hotel's long-ago renovations, the builders found a stray dog and took him in. "That's why their logo is a greyhound." Alicia and I try to listen politely but the lobby takes our breath away—grand and high-ceilinged and perfectly ornate with brocade, marble, gold, and crystal. The bellman shows us to our suite, two rooms with a shared sitting room. L'Wren reaches for her wallet and tips him. "Thank you so much. Will you make sure the reservations for tonight are in order?"

"Of course."

"This room is gorgeous." Alicia is as awestruck as I am. "L'Wren, thank you. *Merci!*" Contemporary and elegant, with Murano glass lighting and tinted oak floors. Alicia twirls in front of the fireplace as if she were home at last.

L'Wren perches on the wide marble step at the suite's entrance, looking wary of accepting Alicia's gratitude. "Diana, I don't mind sharing a room. Should we take this one?" She gestures to a room with two large beds and its own balcony overlooking the hotel's elaborate gardens.

"Don't be silly." Alicia wheels my suitcase toward the shared room. "You upgraded our whole experience. Diana and I can share."

We're now standing in a perfect triangle, 180 degrees of hotel suite marked off among us. All I want is to collapse on a bed and for these two to stop being fake nice.

"Why don't you two share and I'll take my own room?" I don't wait for their reaction. I can hardly believe I've just said it—the room really should be L'Wren's, she did pay for it—but something about Paris has gotten to me. I feel freer somehow, even though we've just gotten here. My friends stand with their mouths agape as I wheel my suitcase into the smaller bedroom. L'Wren claps her hands and calls out, "Okay, but no napping! We're going to power through today and try to get on Paris time!"

Alone in my room, I open the curtains and see the Jardins Tuileries and the tips of chestnut trees across the road. It's so much prettier even than I had ever dreamed. One summer my mother and I spent a full week at the movies, watching only French films. She was trying to become absorbed in *her craft*. My mom loved Jeanne Moreau, aped her every expression. It didn't land my mother any acting gigs, but we were both grateful for the ice-cold air and the large buckets of popcorn. Being here now, I'm surprised by how much of the atmosphere of those films comes back to me.

I unpack my clothes, hanging my sundresses and wondering if L'Wren was right to bring so much luggage. Maybe I should have packed a few more outfits. Alicia calls, "Diana! Meet us downstairs to walk to breakfast in ten. L'Wren and I are starving!"

I should be relieved they have agreed on something. I take a quick, cold shower and put on a creased dress. I check my phone, wanting to call Emmy before she leaves for camp but knowing it's still way too early in Texas. No missed calls from Oliver, which must be a good sign.

At a small café with a blue-painted front, hung with flowers, we sit outside and sip espresso and eat pastries.

"*Petit déjeuner,*" Alicia repeats to herself.

"*Oui. Très bien.*" L'Wren compliments her, somewhat patronizingly. I settle into my chair and take a long sip of my water. The café sits on a hill, and from here I can see the edges of the Fête des Tuileries. I picture Emmy here, us waiting in line for the rides. I imagine the two of us traveling alone—in my mind, I've convinced her to let me sketch her standing in front of the Louvre, her long, wavy hair whipping in front of her face. It's a beautiful image, one I hope to make real, but I feel a niggling gloom. I know what it is—a feeling that someone is missing, but I can't make out who. But why do I have to feel like someone's missing?

I wave my hand in front of my eyes as if to bat away these thoughts. I sit up and take a bite of my croissant. If I keep moving, maybe I won't feel this sadness.

"L'Wren, what's next on the agenda?"

Her eyes light up. "I've taken into account that we're low on sleep, that this will be a first time in the city for both of you, and then I've also considered crowd patterns and weather . . ." She looks up at the sky as if to understand the position of the sun and its bearing on our itinerary. "We'll start at the Arc de Triomphe. Then to the Champs-Elysées and across George V to the Liberty Torch. We'll cross the bridge and stop at Pierre Hermé for macarons and something cold to drink before we get too hot. And then tonight . . . we say yes to it all tonight. . . . Food and champagne and more food . . ."

L'Wren trails off. Her face softens and her eyes go misty, an expression so palpably dreamy she could be joking, like an actor trying to impress us with her uncanny timing. "God, I want to have sex," she murmurs, then blushes when she feels our eyes on her. "Doesn't everyone here look at least a little bit in love?"

We all take a long look around us. The soft sound of other conversations. The facade hung with wisteria so large they need a special city permit.

"You should call your husband." Alicia's voice is gentle. "Have him meet you in Paris for the night. It's just a train ride. Or meet him in London."

"Yeah." L'Wren pulls her focus from the sidewalk and back to the table, looking at me first, then Alicia. "Why doesn't that sound fun?"

"Because you're in love with someone else."

"Alicia!"

"What? Are we not saying it out loud?"

L'Wren sits up taller. Her tone is chilly. "You and I are not saying it, no. We just met yesterday."

Alicia persists. "I'm sorry. I meant—it's totally normal. Expected even. It sounded like a big deal coming out of my mouth, but—really it's not a big deal, it happens."

"It's my marriage. It's my life. *Of course* it's a big deal." L'Wren stares into her coffee.

"I'm so sorry," Alicia says. "But honestly, everyone feels this way in a marriage. Last year I wanted to have sex with my allergist. I kept inventing reasons to go see him."

She gets L'Wren to laugh, which only makes L'Wren's tears fall faster. She wipes them with her napkin. "Did you sleep with him?"

"No. He could not have been less interested in me. I don't know that I actually wanted it to go there. That's the thing—I get your confusion and I'm sorry I sounded overly familiar."

"No, I was being flippant. It's not your fault." She blows her nose into the napkin. "You're right. I do worry that I'm falling for Arthur. And I don't want to."

"Maybe it's just a blip?" I offer.

"No. I definitely want to fuck Arthur. Right here on this table. On the street. In a car."

I am surprised to hear L'Wren open up. My eyes are gritty with fatigue and I'm woozy from caffeine. "Would you, could you in a boat?"

Alicia looks at me and frowns.

"I'm sorry," I say. "Toddler joke. So sorry."

"I would definitely fuck him on a boat," L'Wren says.

"Oh dear."

"I want to. Can I? Just once?"

"L'Wren . . ." I try to sound levelheaded. "It's probably not even about him. Your feelings for Arthur maybe have more to do with you and Kevin. This might have nothing to do with Arthur at all—"

"It *is* about Arthur. He's perfect, Diana. We talk. Like all night on the phone. Kevin and I never talk. Not really. We catch each other up and then we go to bed. I haven't wanted to talk to a man in so long."

I try to catch Alicia's eye, but her gaze, calm and empathetic, is settled squarely on L'Wren. I have no real instinct here, but I do sense L'Wren wants me to make an attempt at advice, at the very least. "Maybe Alicia is right? Maybe you should meet Kevin—somewhere new and far from your everyday lives. You said the same thing to me when I was struggling with Oliver. You said, 'Do everything you can to save your marriage. You don't want any regrets.'"

On our way back to the hotel we stroll arm in arm down a wide, leafy boulevard lined with luxury stores. We pass stunning windowfronts filled with Italian quilted jackets draped over satin slip dresses, gold lambskin loafers, and bold, strange couture looks. Alicia and I exchange a look—if anything could be counted on to lift L'Wren's spirits . . .

"Oh, L'Wren," Alicia says, lingering in front of a short cashmere jacket, "that would be amazing on you."

L'Wren smiles. She sounds pleased. "That red is not quite my color." She points to a metal-studded denim outfit, nudging Alicia. "I can see you in that."

"Gorgeous," Alicia says. "But I have to pee too often to ever wear a jumpsuit."

At the next store, it's me who catches a breath. The dress in the window is so spectacular. It's a deep green with a full skirt. I can't think of any reason I shouldn't have it.

"Wow," is all Alicia says.

"Try it on," L'Wren urges.

"It's probably more than my mortgage." There's a reason.

"I'm only asking you to try . . ." L'Wren says.

We enter the boutique, which is lit by an amazingly quirky bird chandelier. There are worn-in leather club chairs outside of every changing room.

The woman behind the counter is the picture of elegance in a crisp black pantsuit. She has razor-sharp cheekbones and a slick bob. If not for L'Wren's steady hand on my back, I would have turned and run.

"How can I help you?" she asks.

"She'd like to try on the dress in the window," Alicia says.

I feel convinced the saleswoman will know that I cannot afford anything in this store. But she smiles warmly.

"Of course. I'm Marie, if you need anything else."

Alicia starts to actually chant, as though she were at a Texas football game, "Go, Diana, go! Go, Diana, go!"

Inside the mirrored dressing room, I slip on the dress. The full skirt falls just below my knees. I don't recognize my reflection. I feel two feet taller. My skin looks clearer. The dress is transformative. I've spent so many years working in a job where I can melt into the furniture. The woman in the mirror is still *me*—but the me that hasn't been weighed down by an impending divorce, mortgage payments, and first-grade playdates. The woman I see in the mirror has wild sex and is invited to more parties than she can attend.

Marie pops her head into the changing room.

"Gorgeous! But you can't wear it without heels. I'll be right back. Are you a size 7?"

"I am." She's good.

Alicia shouts, "We need to see you!"

"What is the occasion?" Marie asks, returning with a pair of high heels.

I don't have the heart to tell her that I don't have an occasion. I have never had an occasion.

"An evening event," I say lamely.

Seconds later, Marie rests a sleek black blazer over my shoulders.

"Sunglasses?" she asks.

"Yes," I tell her, hiding my ten-dollar gas station frames deep in my purse. She hands me a pair of cat-eye frames.

Before she can ask me about a bag, I leave the dressing room. L'Wren beams.

"Oh. My. God. You are not leaving Paris without that dress."

I do the math in my head. If I never eat out again, quit my weekly tennis lessons for an entire year, and put off replacing the air-conditioning, I can almost afford everything.

"I'll take it," I say. I so desperately want to be this woman. Even if it's just for a few days in Paris.

By late afternoon, we wilt like spent blossoms, our feet swollen and heads woolly and aching. I've bought stacks of postcards for Emmy at every stop along the way, and L'Wren picked up one too— a photo of a kitten in a beret. We spend the evening inside, and I make it until nine P.M., heroically, then give up and sink into the cool linen sheets, my new dress laid out on the king-size bed next to me.

Chapter Six

—

Jet lag wakes me before dawn so I dress quietly and slip out of the hotel. I walk the streets around the neighborhood and then venture farther out, along the Seine and into Le Marais. The sun is just starting to rise. The bistros are gleaming and the cobblestones look wet. I stop to take a picture and without second-guessing myself, I text the photo to Jasper.

Guess where I am. Any chance you'll be passing through?

I slip my phone into my bag and follow the sunlight. It bathes the streets in pale orange and the boulangeries in the quartier are so fragrant, I fill my arms with two baguettes and two pain au chocolat and three warm croissants. Back in the room, I find Alicia and L'Wren awake and sipping espresso. L'Wren is wearing butter-yellow silk pajamas and making notes on the hotel pad. She's on the phone with the concierge.

Alicia is spread out on the floor, stretching her back and reading. "Free time until this afternoon," she whispers. "And we're moving lunch back one hour." She's holding the same book she was so engrossed in on the plane. "You know who this is, don't you?" She sits up and points at the author's name. Sandrine Lemaire. The back cover features a full-length photo of Sandrine, sitting primly on a stool, legs crossed, smiling into the camera. "She's the French Katie Couric. So buttoned-up. But her memoir is insane. It's been translated into a million languages. Very erotic." She tosses it at my feet. "It's dog-eared at all the good parts." I pick it up and admire the simplicity of the plain back cover with the title in tiny gold font. *Playing with Dolls*.

"Research for Dirty Diana." Alicia smiles. She finishes stretching and settles next to me on the couch. "Are you still meeting Petra today?"

I nod, already half absorbed in Sandrine's book. The first page is a list of reviews—sprinkled between raves, the book proudly blurbs some of its own bad press:

Depraved and disgusting enough to win the attention of nitwit fans. Rancid.
Written purely to titillate, devoid of merit.

Alicia peers over my shoulder, smiling. "You should see the online reviews—they're even more entertaining." She scrolls on her phone and reads me her favorites:

"'I read this cover to cover while my lover was on a business trip. It's hilarious that while I was reading, my Apple watch kept reminding me to breathe . . . This memoir was really empowering for me during some hard times . . . An absolute revelation! Love the honesty of her bedroom life . . .'"

"You can borrow it," Alicia tells me. "I'm going to take a shower, then I'm going souvenir shopping for Elvis and eating at every creperie I find along the way."

L'Wren and Alicia leave at the same time, with L'Wren heading to the spa and reminding me, "Have fun with Petra and we'll see you at two."

Alone in our suite, I write a postcard to Emmy, then pace the quiet room, waiting to hear from Petra. After a few minutes, I lie on the couch, holding the book above my head at arm's length. I flip to a random page:

> The process of growing up is understanding that we are not the center of the universe, that other people aren't here to serve us. And that's true! But in fantasy, you can take a break from that, you can even pretend other people are your dolls, that, yes, they are here for nothing but your entertainment. An orgasm is the safest place I find to do that.
>
> Afterward, I emerge, reenergized from my secret depravity, to tidy my kids' bedrooms and be the loving, generous, respectable, socially engaged person that I am during the other twenty-three and a half hours of every day.

My phone chimes with a note from Petra, letting me know she is ready to meet.

Near the fountain. Jardins du Trocadéro.

I take the long route along the Seine and try not to think about the fact that Jasper never replied. I spy a penny candy stand at the end of the block and stop at the rows of vibrantly colored sugar-filled canisters to fill up a bag with gummies. L'Wren will be sure to scold me for buying cheap candy when we're surrounded by the best Parisian chocolatiers, but the sweets remind me of Emmy, and I pop them in my mouth as I make my way to the fountain.

Walking alone in Paris feels dreamlike. Couples gather to dance the tango at one of the amphitheaters that line the Seine. I politely make my way through the small crowd. The men are dressed in crisp button-downs with casual sweaters draped over their shoulders. Not a burnt-orange UT football polo shirt in sight. I'm mesmerized by a couple in all-black clothing who float across the makeshift stage, the man holding perfect form, the woman's head turned dramatically away from him. Applause fills the air.

I pause in the middle of the Pont Alexandre III bridge, which is covered with carvings of cherubs, nymphs, and winged horses. I gaze at the river. The scene takes my breath away. Parisian landmarks are filled with romance, not ego. I watch a photographer take a picture of a bride posing in front of one of the many streetlamps, elegant and lithe in a white silk dress. She is carrying a handful of pale pink roses.

When I finally arrive at the gardens, Petra is easy to spot, sitting on a bench by herself, a large soda and a McDonald's bag by her side.

I can't help my surprise. "Are you eating a Big Mac?"

"Egg McMuffin with cheese. Fry?" She offers me the bag. "Don't look at me like that. It's a tradition. Mitch and I used to come here one June morning every summer and eat McDonald's and look at the blossoms." She grins. "You can take the kids out of Texas . . ."

Her smile quickly fades. I sit beside her, both of us quiet, and follow her gaze to a perfect view of the Eiffel Tower.

"You must miss him every day."

Petra holds out her soda, her eyes still fixed in front of us, and I take a sip. "In the evenings, every hour on the hour, she shimmers for five minutes." Petra cups a hand to her mouth. "Good on you, old Monsieur Eiffel and your steel innovations! What a man. Can you believe that a gigantic gleaming guillotine was the big runner-up idea?"

"That's not true."

"I'm afraid it is. Just when you were ready to start romanticizing another culture's civility, you daffy American!" I take a warm fry from the bag and watch two small kids daring each other closer to the fountain's edge.

She nods. "Mitch liked to know every bit of inconsequential history about a place. All the *what ifs* and *almosts*."

I pull out my notebook and while she tells me about why Mitch wanted to live in Paris, I sketch the sweating soda cup, the straw, and the beginning of her fingers resting on the side of the bench behind it.

Petra glances at my drawing, then looks away. "So, I got you here. Tell me more about what you're making."

I tell her about the interviews I've recorded and how no one, apart from a few people, knows about what I'm making. "Not even my husband. Ex-husband? And one of my best friends has no idea because I've been too chicken to tell her, but she's here in Paris with me, and I still haven't told her. I guess I just have to figure out how to share it, which parts are interesting."

"It's all pretty intriguing, Diana. It makes you that much more interesting."

I laugh, shutting my notebook and stashing it in my bag. "I could be interesting, if only I wasn't working for Allen."

"Debatable." She studies my face, frowning. "I'm sure there are plenty of interesting accountants. But most of them don't make porn. So you just leapfrogged them."

"It's not porn."

"Whatever you call it, I'm intrigued."

"Have you thought at all about the firm?" I ask while Petra is still smiling. The question feels slightly desperate, but I can't seem to shake Allen's look when he asked me for help.

She ignores my question and peppers me with more questions about Dirty Diana and how Liam and I have put it together so far. I describe the site's layout with the portraits I've made of the women with links to their interviews. "And where do you record?" When I tell her I don't have a dedicated space, she frowns. "Have you ever thought of really building the site? Of spending some money and growing an audience. A brand. I *know*, bad word."

"I don't know. I'm still recording fantasies at the office after everyone leaves. Maybe. One day. So far, I'm happy taking baby steps."

"Baby steps are for babies, Diana."

"And we're still in infancy."

She frowns again. "I kinda love that . . . but I also have an extra floor of office space in Dallas. It's just sitting empty. No one's using it and it would be free. I like thinking of someone creating something there."

"Aren't we here to talk about your business?"

"Are we? Boring. Can we not pretend you came all the way to Paris to talk about the firm?"

"Sorry, it's just . . . I kinda did."

She sighs. "Mitch loved Allen and I can honor that."

"So that's it? I can tell Allen?"

"I will give it every serious consideration. Promise." She stands, crumpling her McDonald's bag. "Let's go. I have food shopping to do, and you're coming with." She throws the paper bag into a nearby trash can, and I follow her through the gates of the park.

She loops her arm in mine. "You know, whatever it is you're building, Diana, I could help you."

"Baby steps."

Petra takes me to her favorite green grocer and then to a butcher she greets like an old friend. When we step outside again, I'm conscious of two men approaching.

"Emile!" Petra calls. "This is Emile and his friend, Gabriel. This is Diana."

"Enchanté." Emile has a warm smile. Gabriel is striking, with dark eyes and thick, salt-and-pepper hair. He kisses me on both cheeks, and I feel an immediate attraction.

"It's so nice to meet you both."

Emile turns to Petra and speaks in rapid French before kissing her tenderly on the mouth, then slipping into a clothing store with Gabriel, who glances at me and smiles as he follows Emile inside.

Petra turns to me, a slight blush on her cheeks. "Oh, I forgot you're an American friend. Honestly. I forget. Emile is my secondary. Was. Is?"

"Secondary?"

"Mitch was my primary. And Emile was our secondary. We were in an open marriage."

"Oh. Right. Of course."

"It's okay to be surprised. Everyone expects our show was a full picture."

"Surprised? No! I mean, very cool."

"You're a horrible liar." Petra laughs, both of us looking at our reflection in the store window and just beyond that, Emile and Gabriel hunched over a table of cashmere T-shirts. Petra turns on her heel. "Don't worry, they'll catch up."

"Honestly, whatever works," I say. I hurry to keep pace with her. "I couldn't get one husband to work for me. So."

She isn't really listening, instead snapping a picture of a peach-colored building. "That's the exact paint color I want! For the foyer." She texts the photo to her assistant and keeps walking. "Things have been a little tense since Mitch died. He was the one who really held us together. I didn't know that at the time. But now . . . and I would never tell Emile this, but it all feels a little empty."

"It's still so new," I offer. "I imagine it's very lonely."

She pulls us into the doorway of the next shop, as if to let me know she's done sharing, and tells me, "Mitch loved Emile. And I loved Mitch. And I loved us all together."

After a few more blocks and two more shops, Petra and I make plans to meet for drinks. It occurs to me that I haven't made any solid progress for Allen, but still I casually suggest she extend the drinks invitation to Gabriel and Emile. She smiles knowingly and tells me, "Of course."

I hurry through the busy crowds to my lunch with L'Wren and Alicia. L'Wren has chosen her favorite spot for couscous and we sit at the zinc bar, eating tagine and drinking cold beer. When we get back to the room, I lie down for a nap but end up diving back into Sandrine Lemaire's memoir.

Ever since I first started making my own money, I only ever cared about spending it on girlie things: touchable fabrics, tea dresses, high heels, stockings, and, after my divorce, pretty wallpaper, curtains, and carpets, in shades of rose and cream. And yet the thing that brought me the most pleasure to contemplate? Other beautiful women—the girlier the better.

This longing to have sex with doll-like women has been with me since I was a schoolgirl. Being short, brunette, and an outsider, I was excluded from the clique I most wished to join, an array of blondes, all of them scented like fruit lip gloss. These girls were all slender and had trimmed the skirts of their school uniforms to mere inches below their little bubble butts. I found them to be idiotic, cartoonish, and awkward, parroting vapid gestures they had no experience of. But I would have given anything for the spotlight of their attention to fall on me. I was invisible to them. If they did notice me, it was only to mock my outfits and interests.

I never saw these girls again after the age of eighteen. But from the time I turned twenty, when I first started sleeping with men, my erotic imagination bound those girls' wrists behind their backs while I had sex with them.

I was incredibly turned on by these fantasies. I found myself drawn to men with cocks so large and so thick that I could allow myself to imagine them as extensions of my own body. *That's my erection now,* I'd think, *and I am going to use it.* But to be clear, I never wanted to make tender love to any girl about whom I'd fantasize. I wanted to hold her hair by the topknot, tip back her head, and kiss her roughly. These girls are my dolls to play with.

I flip the book over and study Sandrine's author photo again. Her perfect posture. Her pantyhose. Her perfectly blown-out hair and small, ordinary smile. I would not have pictured her like this. I'm fascinated by the disconnect.

When the man I was sleeping with was pushing and grunting and moving around inside of me, I'd tell my fantasy girl, *You don't have to move. Stay still.* You see, a boy I once slept with had said this exact phrase to me, and his words had made me feel awful, as if I didn't even need to be there, not really. But I liked to imagine these words emerging from my own mouth. I liked to imagine the terrible looks on my girls' faces when they felt both ashamed and aroused. Or when they felt manipulated and confused because they were so shocked by the ways I found to turn them on. With my deep voice, I'd whisper filth in their delicate seashell ears. All the things that had been said to me in the years I had been having sex, when I was young and vulnerable, I now said to these dolls, even when I masturbated. "I'm only going to put the tip in," I'd say before I tricked them. I turned them over and around into shapes they hadn't been meant to bend into. Tough, baby, you're my doll.

I kept having these fantasies as I got older, even after I married my first husband, and they only intensified after our separation. I never want to be cruel or degrading to any woman, let alone someone younger and more vulnerable than me. But in my fantasies, my power is my greatest pleasure. My ex-husband once said that every time he'd dated a woman with a younger sister, she'd had these same instincts. He'd done more sexual exploring than I had and had had many threesomes with his ex-girlfriend who, big sister that she was, had always wanted the other girl to be treated rough.

I don't ever want to be the doll. I don't want to be played with, I want to do the playing. I want to be the puppeteer. But I am a woman, so that isn't handed to me. Less and less so the older I get. I don't want to be put on the shelf or discarded. I do this to the girls in my head like an offering to the gods so that it doesn't happen to me.

I rest the book on my chest. Alicia has folded over the corners of every page that describes a sexual encounter and now the book is bulging. I assume a good part of the book is like this. Not the memoir people must have expected. Maybe because of how graphic it is—or maybe because she never apologizes for it. There is no mention of being one way for the public and another in private, she just is. I fall asleep thinking about Dirty Diana and its total absence of *me*. I ask women questions I never ask myself. Should I be sharing more? And if I did share a fantasy, what would it be? I'm inspired by the way Sandrine opens up, as if nothing is off-limits. She makes herself vulnerable while I'm hiding behind my sketches.

I wake up with just enough time to shower and meet Petra. L'Wren and Alicia are on the couch drinking wine. Alicia is playing Edith Piaf through her phone's tinny speaker and L'Wren is wearing her cheap felt beret from Alicia.

"Diana!" Alicia jumps up and hugs me. "How was your nap?"

"Good." I think of inviting them for drinks though it's clear they have a head start. "Are you in for the night?"

"What night?" L'Wren asks, hugging me too. Up close I see their eyes are glassy and stoned. "You mean tonight? Not tomorrow night—no, that wouldn't make any sense." L'Wren breaks the hug and holds Alicia by the wrist. "Are you this stoned or is it just me?"

"I'm barely stoned. I can totally still do this." Alicia twirls and bows at the exact same time our hotel doorbell chimes, which they both find hilarious.

"Room service!" L'Wren shrieks. Instead of opening the door, she runs to the mirror and applies lipstick. Alicia calls her on it and they start laughing again, still not answering the door.

"I'll get it." I let the waiter in and he spends the next several minutes removing silver lids from plates, revealing dish after dish—delicate sea scallops covered in leeks, an enormous cheeseburger, an entire plate of fries, and a neat row of cheeses. L'Wren and Alicia watch his every move in quiet awe.

When he leaves, they dig in.

"So that's a yes, you're in for the evening?"

"We love you so much, Diana." L'Wren dips a cornichon in mustard and eats it in one bite.

"Yes," Alicia agrees. "But you'll have mooch more fun out on the town. Did I just say 'mooch'?"

I decide to wear my new dress to meet Petra for drinks. I can't think of a single occasion in Rockgate that would call for a dress this special, so I pair it with the blazer and head out the door.

In the elevator, I get a text from Jasper. Just the sight of his name on my phone gives me a rush.

Just saw your text. You're in Paris!

I wait until I'm in the street to respond. *I'm here. Very happy to be. I'm sure the last thing you need is more on your itinerary but . . .*

I break into a grin. He's coming to meet me.

. . . *my good friend Fred has a show on in the 9th arr. It's sort of . . . unmissable.*

My heart sinks. I walk for several minutes, watching my phone and waiting for the part where he tells me if he'll be there too. When nothing more comes in, I type, *Sounds like I have to see it.*

He hearts the message and then disappears.

Petra is already at the café, at a table squeezed in close next to Emile, and she applauds when I walk in. "Paris looks very good on you!" She beams and I catch Gabriel taking me in. It's crowded and we shout happily to be heard. Petra makes sure we're never without a drink, and Emile runs across the road to the *tabac.* I haven't felt this blissfully stupid while drunk since high school. A tingling sensation runs through me—an overwhelming sense of relief that I don't need to lay eyes on Jasper to feel this happy in Paris.

The more Petra has to drink, the longer she rests her head on Emile's shoulder. He kisses her hair every few minutes and she sighs dreamily. When she does, I catch Gabriel's eye and we both smile. The warmth of Petra and Emile is contagious, and I get more and more excited each time Gabriel inches his chair closer to mine or leans closer to whisper in my ear instead of shout.

Emile tells me about the first time he and Petra met—it was in a crowded café like this one and he noticed Mitch and Petra right away. But the crowd was thick and he was sure they'd disappear soon. A few minutes later, he looked up from his drink and Mitch was standing over his table. Mitch introduced himself and asked for his number. They flirted for just a moment before he returned to Petra's side. And then, moments later, Petra sent Emile a suggestive photo.

"How suggestive?" I ask, the warmth of Gabriel's knee touching mine beneath the table.

"A bit of her naked shoulder." Emile smiles. "Maybe a little more."

This sets us off joking about how to take a sexy picture and fooling around with our phones. Everybody starts with exaggerated pouts into the camera, then the men flex their muscles and send the photos to each other, laughing. After my third drink, I wander to the bathroom and without letting myself grow chicken, I take a picture of my naked breasts and text it to Gabriel. When I get back to the table, he smiles at our shared secret, then pulls out my chair, scooting it closer to his, and drapes an arm across my shoulders. I breathe in the scent of his musky cologne mixed with the gin on his breath.

Another friend of Emile's appears and Petra and Emile peel off with him, kissing us good night. Petra gives me an easy smile. "Catch up tomorrow?"

Gabriel asks if I'm hungry. "We can go for Indian. Can you bear no little bistro?"

I don't want the evening to end.

He takes us to a place not far from the Boulevard Saint-Germain. When the host seats us, Gabriel ignores the banquette across from mine and slides in next to me. The room is crowded and buzzy—no longer so loud that we need to shout—and it's nice to share the same view and to take it in together.

The champagne is cold and I feel it in my chest. A waiter in his long white apron nearly collides with another.

"So you've always lived in the States?"

"I grew up in California. Then New Mexico, briefly. Now Texas is home."

"Where everything is bigger?"

"Exactly. And you said you're an agent?"

"Yes. Writers mostly. Some actors."

"Do you have kids?"

"Two. At university. You?"

"One. Seven years old."

"You have a lot to look forward to."

"I feel that way."

"And you're enjoying Paris?"

"Yes, very much. And we have so many plans."

"Tell me."

I whip through some of L'Wren's itinerary and he laughs. "It's a lot, but you should enjoy every minute. I love to travel. I go to New York every spring; I should look you up. How far is Rockgate from Manhattan?"

"I'm sorry." I laugh. "I'm trying to picture you in a town with two Walmarts."

"You never know." He leans in close, brushing the hair from my neck and kissing my shoulder. My cheeks flush.

I turn my face so that my lips brush his. He kisses me and runs his hand through my hair.

He pulls away and whispers in my ear, "So how do you feel now?"

"Not as hungry."

We sit against the banquette, both looking out over the room. He puts a hand on my leg. The waiter sets a curry in front of us.

"I know what you want." Gabriel slides a hand down my thigh, over my skirt until it finds the hem, just above my knee. "But first you have to tell me." He stops there, asking permission. In response, I let my legs fall slightly open, letting my knee rest against his. A rush of excitement courses through me.

The waiter brings over the last side dish, a tamarind rice. The plate hits with a soft thud. He straightens the tablecloth and walks away.

Gabriel turns to look at me, his eyes warm. Then he settles against the backrest and picks up his wineglass. The hand under the table is gently stroking my skin. "Tell me again," he says.

"I want you to touch me."

Slowly, his hand moves up the side of my bare thigh. My skin grows hot beneath his touch, a warmth quickly spreading from my stomach to between my legs.

I continue staring straight ahead as his fingertips lightly brush against the warm skin of my thighs. I take another sip of cold champagne, set the glass down, and let my hand fall over his. I tug my underwear aside. He glides his fingers inside me. From afar we look like a lived-in couple, making an effort to leave the house and spend an evening dining together. But beneath the table, he is exploring me with his fingers and the thrill is, of course, that we are new to each other.

The waiter approaches the table once more and I make my whole body still; Gabriel continues to push his fingers inside me, speaking to the waiter in rapid French. The waiter turns to me and I dip my head, shifting my hips, feeling a sharp secret explosion of pleasure as Gabriel straightens up, pulling the silk fabric back into place, lifting his arm onto the table and laying it over mine as if nothing happened at all.

The waiter fills my glass and leaves. I feel like a teenager again. My face is burning. Gabriel grins. He begins spooning food onto our plates. "Will you try it all? You are all right with spicy?"

After dinner, Gabriel walks me along the bank of the Seine. He invites me back to his apartment. It's simple and tasteful. A tufted velvet chair in the corner. Blankets resting on a plush couch. He sets the Moka pot on the stove for coffee.

A cat jumps onto my lap. Gabriel walks back and forth to the tiny kitchen, preparing coffee and whiskey and oranges. He sits down across from me.

He rubs at his face. He settles into a chair. His voice is soft. "It's nice to have you here. I was so glad to have a good reason not to go to an event I was supposed to attend tonight." An ottoman covered in an old kilim sags under stacks of books and scripts.

I watch him, poised, long legs crossed on the coffee table. It's not unnerving for him, I don't think, to be so physically intimate with someone so fast. He moves easily between modes. It's sort of thrilling.

"You want milk?" He's very attentive.

He stands over my chair and we laugh over the photos we sent back and forth. He kisses my neck and tugs on the straps of my dress. I help him, cinching the top of my dress down to my waist. "I like this one." He takes my phone and shows me the photo. "I like to see this part of your neck, and then the breast and then just a bit of nipple, not too much."

I open my bra and take the phone so I can snap another photo. He cups both my breasts, kissing me and lifting me out of the chair. We play like this in his living room, taking pictures of each other. The room spins and I feel young. On his couch, I lie on my back as he kisses my calves, then my knees. I aim a shot at the slope of my stomach and my fingers in my own dark pubic hair pulling tight the fabric of my underwear so it bites into my skin. He slips an arm under me and pulls me up, kissing me all the way to his bed.

My heart races. I didn't think I would have a first time with someone, ever again. Even the way he looks at me is different. A confident intensity, as if he knows exactly what he wants to do to me. When we're both naked, he sits on the edge of his bed and pulls me onto his lap. We have sex like this, moving and moaning into each other's mouths. I tilt my head back as he kisses my neck and I smile, catching a glimpse of his unfamiliar bedroom. A stranger's things, the feel of a stranger's lips, a strange city. My new dress like a crumpled flower on his bedroom floor.

We fall back on his bed, first catching our breath, then going quiet. I enjoy the heat of his body next to mine. I lie like this for what feels like hours, watching the sky lighten through his bedroom windows, feeling the sweat on the skin of his arm, his soft breathing.

"I can make coffee."

"No, go back to sleep."

We kiss goodbye and I tell him how much I enjoyed myself. I walk back to the hotel, dreamy and bathed in morning light. I think about the reader reviews to Sandrine's book and make up my own about last night:

Went in not knowing what to expect and was pleasantly surprised!

The positions worked nicely for both of us. Three and a half out of four stars!

I totally lost myself! Much like Diana did between the sheets!

I entertain myself like this the entire walk back to the hotel.

Chapter Seven

I gently crack open the door to our suite and creep inside, relieved to find it quiet, aside from some light snoring coming from L'Wren and Alicia's room. I sink onto the edge of my bed and kick off L'Wren's heels. It's dangerous to sit too long—I need to get in the shower before I fall asleep. My feet ache and even my skin feels sensitive and tight. I take a deep breath but before I can push myself up and into the bathroom, my phone vibrates beside me. Oliver is FaceTiming. My mind races—it's almost midnight in Dallas. Emmy. Something must be wrong.

"Hello?"

Oliver asks, "How's Paris?"

"Amazing."

"Did I wake you up?"

"No . . . I . . . Jet lag."

"And L'Wren?"

"In her element. And fast asleep."

"Well." Oliver leans deeper into the couch, one arm folded beneath his head. I remember the feeling of being nestled in the crook of that arm, warm and safe, my head on his chest, listening to his heartbeat. "I miss you."

I see myself in the tiny FaceTime square, my eyes puffy from champagne and with the last of yesterday's makeup. "Thank you for getting Emmy off to camp. How did it go?"

"Fine. Easy." Oliver runs his hand across his face, suddenly looking very tired. "I told you once you were there we would slip away and you would enjoy every second."

"I am. It's hard to think about Emmy so far away. But I do love it here."

Oliver's smile is small and sad. "Diana . . ."

"Yeah . . ."

"You sent me a picture earlier. And I don't think it was for me."

Oh god. "What?"

"Check your phone."

No. No. No. Please god no. I couldn't have. I couldn't have been so careless. Did I send a picture to Oliver?

Oh. My. God. There it is. Me on Gabriel's couch, underwear pulled aside.

"I don't know what to say."

"So it wasn't for me?"

"I am so sorry."

"Don't be. Really. It's fine. It's nothing I haven't seen before."

My entire face is hot and red. A long moment passes. Neither of us is brave enough to speak. Until finally Oliver asks, in a quiet voice, "You want to know what I kept thinking about? After I got the picture?"

No. Not really. I'd rather bury myself under these pillows. Is that an option?

"We never sent pictures like this to each other."

I race for something to say—but my mind is still stuck on the photos—how did I make such a stupid mistake?

"Right. Anyway. It's late here. I should go to bed. Sleep well."

We never sent pictures like this to each other. It was the last thing I expected him to say.

"You too."

I lie down in my clothes, on top of the sheets, until I hear L'Wren and Alicia stir, padding through the suite getting ready. L'Wren had insisted she'd only do the Louvre if we go bright and early, before the major crowds. They are both up and showered by eight A.M., and I do my best to join them, but then they take one look at me—still in last night's clothes with heavy shadows under my eyes—and they tell me to go right back to bed. They head out on their own, and I shower finally and fall asleep, hard and fast. I don't wake up until one in the afternoon and only then because Alicia is standing over me with a cup of coffee.

"I'm waking you now so you don't mess up your biorhythm entirely," she says.

"Where's L'Wren?" I ask, groggily.

"L'Wren has declared me a 'delight' if a little 'unfiltered.' And she's decided I walk too slow, so we're not a good fit for shopping. We were a couple blocks from the hotel and she mumbled something about Hermès and then disappeared into a taxi." Alicia flops onto the Louis XVI–style settee at the end of the bed. "She is really a trip."

I pull a pale blue sundress over my head. "I'm just relieved you're getting along."

"I get along with everyone, eventually."

Alicia takes me to La Grande Mosquée de Paris. We pass through a courtyard, shaded in foliage where the last of the season's wisteria blooms cling to the archways, and into the Turkish baths. Inside it's busy, crowded with naked women all in different states of repose. A group of older women sit by the edge of the Jacuzzi, sweating and dipping their feet in and out of the water, none of them self-conscious. I drop my towel and join Alicia on the soft green mats. She takes the bar of black soap we've each been given and motions for me to turn around. She gently scrubs between my shoulders where she knows I can't reach. Then she turns so I can do the same to her.

Afterward, we sit in the café drinking sweet mint tea and eating pistachio pastries. I sketch the place on the back of one of my post-cards so I won't forget it. Alicia tilts her head up to the late-afternoon sun and closes her eyes. Her voice is soft and dreamy. "I'm never going back, Diana. Never."

"Should I let your husband know?"

"I'm serious. Do I have to go back?"

"You can't fool me. I know how much you miss Nico and Elvis."

"It's crazy though, isn't it? That when you're in it, you're so *in it*. You can't imagine leaving even for a day, you'll miss your family too much. But then you do leave and you can be so out of it. Instantly. I thought being away from Elvis would feel like missing a limb. Instead I feel like I'm completely in my body. Like it's all mine again."

I clasp my hand over hers and give her fingers a light squeeze. "Everyone needs a break."

"Last night, I sat on the couch in the hotel room and no one asked me for a single thing. Not a glass of water. Or a snack. Not help wiping a butt or turning on an iPad. No one asked me if I knew where their *fill-in-the-blank-with-literally-anything* was. I miss being totally selfish and only thinking about satisfying the exact craving I'm having and at the exact moment I'm craving it. If I feel like working, I work. If I'm hungry, I eat." She stretches her arms over her head and closes her eyes again. "I love that L'Wren has a massive crush on someone. But that's my nightmare right now. Can you imagine taking on one more person's *feelings* right now? Good for her and also *no thank you*."

She lets out a long sigh and we pay the bill, wandering to the nearby park and finding two chairs in a shady spot under a tree. Alicia closes her eyes and dozes off, and I stay still, reading and not wanting to wake her.

My phone chimes as I turn the page. Jasper.

So, Diana's in Paris. What does she do next?

I don't hesitate:

What doesn't she do?

For a few moments, there is no response from him, and then:

Hmm . . .

I watch the three dots linger, then disappear.

Chapter Eight

—

At lunch the next day, L'Wren announces that she has decided to take our advice and surprise Kevin. "I'm taking my new Chanel bag on an impromptu trip to London! *Not* homework, right? But don't have too much fun without me." Shortly after she leaves, Alicia and I get on a Zoom call with Liam, who wants to show me a new Dirty Diana layout idea.

"This is just a beta version," he tells us, sharing his screen.

"Okay, what am I looking at exactly?" I narrow my eyes and study the screen.

"Your work—each piece is featured here—and down below a button to click play."

"Is it odd just to stare at one piece while we listen?" Alicia asks.

"That's what I thought," he says. "But I like that it's lo fi."

"Can it spin?"

"Have you ever visited a website?"

"I know but—what skills have we got?"

"We'll find someone who knows Animator."

"What's that?"

"Not to worry, we got this," Alicia says. "But how fancy?"

"I'm not sure. I have these four small sketches, which I plan to paint." I run to get my sketchbook and show them what I've been drawing in Paris, still works in progress.

"Diana. Holy shit." Liam approves.

"These are stunning."

"Thanks, you two."

"You'll tell me which fantasy goes with which?"

I nod as Alicia asks, "Can we feature all of them?"

"Can they look like they are clipped to a bookstall?" I add. "Edges moving?"

"I like that idea," Liam says.

"Like they're for sale along the Seine," murmurs Alicia.

In the early evening, Alicia and I decide to wander the city without a plan. We visit Bon Marché, riding the grand elevators and people watching. She catches me looking too often at my phone and I confess that Jasper had texted about a friend's show and that it wasn't far from where we were.

"Will Jasper be there?" she asks me.

My cheeks flush. "No. He's in London."

She looks at me, hardly blinking.

"Alicia, it's his *friend's* show."

There are only a few other people in the art gallery, and the atmosphere is very friendly. We're in two brightly lit rooms that had to be accessed through a loud brasserie, and the feeling is intimate.

I scan the small canvases in the front room. A woman comes from behind a desk to offer me a glass of wine and show me the paintings in the next room. How did I hear about the exhibit? I tell her that I know Jasper Green and that he had said not to miss it.

Alicia has struck up a conversation with a man named Paul who went to school in Greece and Argentina. They slip into fluent Spanish and then back to English.

Another man in a pale blue shirt approaches us. A little scar on his upper lip. "This is our artist, Frederic," the woman says, and he, too, is happy to hear that I was sent by Jasper.

Frederic asks me what I've been doing in Paris, and when I describe my days, he seems unimpressed. Have I seen the Cal Tiezen exhibition around the corner? he wants to know; it's a very tiny place, even smaller than this.

Overhearing this, another woman joins us and groans. "Not that shithead."

"Yes, I know, Fidelle." Frederic frowns. "Tiezen is very much not in fashion right now but the big canvases are so close, and the room is so tiny—it is worth seeing it while they are here."

Now there are only a handful of us remaining in the gallery, and the attention turns to me and Alicia, the newest visitors to Paris. The group decides to take us for a drink nearby, to their new favorite spot.

We walk a few blocks to a small bar even though it's begun to drizzle. It's a narrow wood-paneled room with vinyl tables, ugly yellow lamps, and long white candles. A man brings around the house drink on a round tray, some sort of jellied liqueur with a dollop of cream.

Tinkling piano music starts up, and a rouged-cheeked, dark-haired woman is singing from one of the corners, and then she gathers force in her voice and really sings, wandering up to a small stool in front of the bar, a cigarette in her mouth.

"This is the most Parisian a night can get." Alicia beams. But after our second round of drinks, she declares she's beat and ready for bed.

I should leave, too, but I feel a pull to stay as I am still wide awake. "See you back at the hotel?"

Fidelle and Paul and I coax the singer into a few more songs, which she obliges, smiling and clinking our short glasses, while Frederic is smoking, deep in conversation with the bartender. Behind me I hear the door scrape and suddenly there is Jasper. We all stand to greet him as he kisses Fidelle and shakes hands with Frederic and then he's next to me.

"Found you," he says, smiling, hands in his jeans pockets.

My heart is in my throat, my pulse pounding. Any pretending I've been doing that it's okay if I don't get to see him on this trip falls away. I'm exactly where I want to be, with exactly whom I want to be with. I break into a grin. "Found me. Having a night out in Paris." I try to calm my sudden nerves, waving my hand around the small room and playing as if this is the most normal thing in the world, him and me, together at this bar. "I liked Frederic's show very—"

He pulls me close and kisses my cheek. If I could wish for anything, I would stop time. Extend this moment so I can revel in it longer and revisit it years from now, still sharply in focus. The surprise of it all. The feel of his cheek against mine. The effortless stubble and tussled hair. His dimpled smile.

He takes me by the hand and leads me to the bar. We sit on two stools, our legs touching. His arm brushing against mine, both of us looking straight ahead, into the mirror behind the bar. "Good, right? Fred's show?"

"Very."

Jasper turns to me and exhales. "Diana in Paris . . ."

I shift my body to face his. "Now that you have me here . . ."

"I wish it weren't so late already. I left my dinner early but you weren't at the gallery. Then I tried the bar across the road. I wanted to surprise you."

"You did."

"Tell me. What have you seen so far?"

I pull a handful of postcards from my purse. "The Pompidou, the Arc de Triomphe, of course . . ." I can feel him looking at me. He takes one of the cards and asks the bartender for a pen. "I'll write one for you. I think I can capture your voice." He jots something on the card and slips it back into my purse. "I'm sure I'll regret that later." He grins. "What else can I show you?"

"Show me . . . anything new, I guess. New places and streets."

"That is something I can do." He lowers his voice. "God, I'm glad I found you."

Jasper swings a bottle of champagne he took from the bar as we walk arm in arm through the narrow streets. Most businesses are shut up tightly for the night, but when we pass any place still open, Jasper buys me something new—an ice cream, a key chain, a peach-tinted lip balm, a lighter shaped like the Eiffel Tower—until my pockets are full of new trinkets. At one point, he stops suddenly in the middle of the road. He looks at me like he used to just before he took my picture. And then he goes silent.

My mind races. How many women has he dated since we were together? Does he often take them to Paris? Does he just want to fuck me? Does he want to marry me? What is his five-year plan? I can't remember the last time I cared about any of these things.

I think of tense car rides to work with Oliver, bickering over something forgettable. Or the way one of us would fall into a familiar story, knowing the information felt stale and the other couldn't care less. With Jasper, information is charged, every detail exciting. I want to know everything.

As a car approaches, I grab for his hand but he doesn't move. "What if we tried again?" he asks me. "Do you think it's possible?"

I don't say anything. I don't know. I take his other hand and this time he follows me onto the sidewalk.

"I'm so happy to see you here, Diana. You have no idea." He closes the space between us.

As soon as his body touches mine, I'm twenty-six again. Carefree. I want to scream from the roof of my hotel, *Yes! Let's try again. Try even harder. Fuck all the heartbreak.*

Without thinking, I pull him away from the streetlight and into the dark space between two buildings, a gap narrower than an alley-way. There is nothing timid about the way I kiss him, pressing him up against the brick wall, still wet with rain. His mouth meets mine with equal force. "Diana," he says, then breaks away. He takes my face in his hands.

Out of the corner of my eye, I watch a young couple hurry across the road. We're just out of sight of everyone. Standing on my toes, I find his mouth again. He tastes like champagne and smells like the rain and we're all over each other, hurriedly, like if we move too slowly the desire might evaporate. His hands on me feel familiar and foreign all at once. We can't really be here, together, after so long. One of us must be dreaming. I press into him. Jasper lifts my skirt and I wrap my legs around him. My breathing quickens. I want him inside me so badly. I've lost control.

"Touch me," I tell him. I lean into the wall for balance as he slides his hand between my legs. I want him to feel how excited I am. The sound of sirens in the distance. The lights of Paris above us. I feel dizzy from it all.

"Diana . . . I only want to be right here, with you."

I unbutton Jasper's jeans and take him in my hand, hard and throbbing. He moans as I glide his erection between my legs, moving back and forth until my body opens for him. He lifts me up and pushes deep inside me. My fingers are digging into his neck. I feel his open mouth on my bare shoulder.

He's here. He's where he should be. It's all I can think. After all these years he feels the same. Strong and solid, gentle and assured. His breathing is ragged too. The sensation is sending us both over the edge. How could I ever have settled for less than this feeling? How could I have forgotten that he was made for me?

"Is this okay?" he asks.

I tighten my legs around him as we build a delicious rhythm. He pushes inside me so hard, moving in and out so slowly that unrecognizable sounds come from my mouth. A bliss I didn't know I could feel.

We freeze when we hear footsteps nearby. I close my eyes and bite gently on his finger to quiet my heavy breathing. Jasper moves his body to shield mine. The footsteps pass.

"We should be in a bed," he says.

"I couldn't wait for a bed."

He moves inside me and I feel him grow even harder.

"Tell me how much you missed it," he says.

"I missed it," I moan. "Jasper. I could stay like this forever." I could. How different sex could be with Jasper. I couldn't imagine dreading it, having to schedule it. All I want is for this feeling to last longer.

But for a moment, Jasper stops. He hitches me up higher on his hips and looks into my eyes. His hand, wet from pressing onto the rain-soaked wall, gently strokes my cheek. He feels it too. The intensity of being thrown back in time. Of remembering how good we can make each other feel. If we do this—if we keep going—neither of us can lie to ourselves anymore about what we're missing when we're apart.

"Jasper—"

The sound of a glass bottle being kicked down the street. A group of strangers laughing, their feet slapping the ground as they run. We could be caught at any moment.

"Please," I tell him. "I need more."

He smiles, his mouth on mine, kissing me hungrily as he pushes deeper into me. I arch my back so he can go farther. His breath against my neck. The feeling of his bare skin, of him moving inside me, faster and faster. There is no warning. An explosion of heat between my legs and he feels it too. My grip tightens on his shoulders. He kisses me as I cry out in pleasure and he comes with me.

We both are reeling as we walk back to my hotel. We stay quiet, silently marveling over what just happened, one of us stopping every few feet to kiss the other. It takes us fifteen minutes to walk the few short blocks back to the hotel.

At the hotel entrance he announces, "I'm walking you to the elevator." We make it through the lobby doors, both still weak in the knees.

"What time am I picking you up tomorrow?"

"Jasper. Tomorrow's our last day in Paris. We fly out on Saturday."

"But what if you stayed? Just the weekend. I'm here until Monday."

He tips my chin and kisses me gently. "I need more Diana in Paris. I have things to show you. Spend tomorrow with your friends and see them off, and then Saturday morning, you're all mine, the entire weekend." When I smile, he blushes. "Diana, you've seen everyone else's favorite Paris but you haven't seen mine."

Yes. Yes, I will stay a few extra days in Paris. Yes, I will lie to Allen and tell him how close I am to getting Petra to keep her money with the firm. Yes, I will also lie to Oliver and tell him Petra's schedule is impossible and our meeting got rescheduled and I'll be home on Monday instead. Yes. Yes. Yes.

Jasper kisses me good night and fades away through the lobby's revolving doors. Before I get into bed, I find the postcard he slipped into my purse and read his note:

To whom it may concern: I've extended my stay in Paris. Remember Jasper? Tallish. Massively charming. Great cock. Takes photos. He's the reason. God, I love Paris. Diana x

I wake up to the sound of crying coming from the sitting room, the morning light bright and white across my bed. I hurry out of bed toward Alicia's voice, soothing and calm. I find her comforting L'Wren, who is sitting on the couch in a sea of French drugstore beauty products.

"Oh no. What happened?" I join them, my hand touching L'Wren's knee.

"Nothing. A big fat nothing happened."

"Her night in London was a bust."

"Kevin was on the phone the entire time. I took the first train back this morning and spent three thousand dollars on French drugstore products on my way back to the hotel. I don't even know how I'm going to get them home." She looks from one of us to the other, a cry hitching in her throat. "This one is really good for cellulite by the way." She holds up a white-and-silver box.

"Did you tell Kevin how important this night was to you?"

"Yes. Between phone calls. At one point he told me to email his assistant next time I want to surprise him; he asked how I could be upset if this wasn't on the schedule."

"L'Wren. We gave you shaky advice—it was a lot of pressure to put on one night."

"Oh please. It's a symptom of a much bigger problem. A problem I've been too scared to face."

"It's time to call the veterinarian. I give you full permission." Alicia holds her hand. "You really tried."

L'Wren looks so vulnerable, like she'll follow any orders she's given. "But don't I have to try like ten more times?"

"How long have you been trying before this night?"

"I don't know. Honestly, I stopped keeping track."

"When was the last time you had sex?"

"Sex isn't the problem with us. Kevin can't seem to prioritize talking for longer than five minutes, but we know how to have good sex."

L'Wren's phone chimes on the table. "If it's Kevin, I'm not responding." When she looks at the screen, her whole face lights up. "Oh my god. It's Miss Ginger. His office cat. Drinking from a water fountain." L'Wren laughs into her tissue, then wipes her nose. "Arthur and I never run out of things to talk about. He's genuinely interested when I talk." She shows off all the recent cat pictures he's sent.

"Okay, but for a minute let's forget about Arthur," I say. "Pretend he's out of the picture. He doesn't exist. How do you feel about Kevin? What would you miss?"

"Why are you so pro my marriage?"

"I'm not. I just . . . sometimes things you miss sneak up on you. So you have to throw it all in the mix, the good and the bad, and sort through. That's what we're here for. Use us."

"Full disclosure," Alicia admits. "I'm strong Team Adorable Vet at the moment."

"You've never met Kevin."

"I'm just saying, yes, let's sort, for sure, but I'm feeling a strong bias. But yes, Diana's right, let's think about what you'd miss most."

"Oh come on. If I say 'money,' you'll both be turned off by me. But I like the money. We'd all be staying at a French Red Roof Inn right now if it wasn't for Kevin."

"I'm not judging. I appreciate this room and this robe very much. But what else?"

"It's not just the money. It's the ambition. His drive. I like his ambition and I'm completely repelled by it at the same time. That's how fucked-up I am. He can't win. So maybe this is my fault?"

"Don't do that. He's been neglectful and it hurts."

"I just want to be in love again. I've made up too many excuses for Kevin. He's never emotionally available. I want to feel excited to be near someone and feel like they don't want to be anywhere else in the world either, except with me."

Alicia grabs a fresh box of tissues from the bathroom and sits on the couch next to L'Wren, their knees touching. L'Wren leans into her. "You know, there is such a thing as too emotionally available. Sometimes I wish Nico would just leave his feelings at the door—I actually say that to myself in my head. He likes to have at least two check-ins every day. And by the way, 'fine' and 'good' are not *feeling words,* so there are no shortcuts."

"That sounds kinda nice. Kevin is too checked out for a check-in. Meeting Arthur just brought it all to the surface. It's like now I know what it's supposed to feel like. The secret is out, you know? And I can't imagine going back to how it felt with Kevin."

"What do you want to do?"

"Honest answer? Run away with Arthur and move to a little island with him and Halston. You two could visit, of course. But the dreams I have about Arthur are so intense. Every time I think about him, I'm turned on. I'm not kidding, I would drink his bathwater. Every drop."

"Hmm." I can see Alicia trying to compute the urge without judgment. "Would you drink Kevin's?"

L'Wren gives this serious thought. "He is very clean. So. Maybe I'd sip it."

L'Wren's shoulders dip and her head sinks between them. Alicia smooths her hair until she stops crying again. She really does get along with everyone, eventually.

"There is nothing worse than feeling lonely in a city where everyone around you is in love." L'Wren groans into Alicia's robe.

"I'm not in love," I offer.

This gets a "ha" from them both.

"You are too." L'Wren laughs. "You have so many feelings running through you right now you don't know what to do with them."

I sit on the floor at their feet and tell them about Jasper showing up at the bar last night.

"Dammit," Alicia says, "I left too early. I knew he'd show up! Then what?"

I recount our stroll through the city and when I get to the part about the end of our walk, I pause.

"And?" Alicia asks.

And he kissed me on the cheek and we said good night . . . It would be so easy to end the story there.

"And I pulled him into a dark corner near the hotel and we had sex against a wall."

For a moment, the room is quiet. L'Wren looks from Alicia to me and back to Alicia. "Is she telling the truth?"

Alicia laughs. *"Thank god I left when I did!"*

"Diana!" L'Wren grabs my hand, and for a brief moment I worry a lecture is coming. *"This is what I mean—the way you feel right now. I want this."*

Alicia and I hug L'Wren tight. "We're going to figure it out," I tell her. "You're not in this alone."

"Absolutely not alone," Alicia agrees. "Just think, tonight we can crawl into bed and snuggle with your French beauty products. They might not even all fit in the bed."

L'Wren laughs and blows her nose into a fresh tissue.

"But first, we'll have our last day in Paris," Alicia tells me. "Except for you. You should stay."

"Neither of you will be upset if I change my ticket?"

L'Wren narrows her eyes. "As long as we can go somewhere really trendy for dinner tonight that doesn't take reservations and we might have to wait forever."

"Of course!"

For the rest of the day, Alicia and I do our best trying to cheer L'Wren up. We open every one of her beauty products and sample them on her. Then we wrestle them all into her luggage and go for an early dinner at an open-air kitchen inside the Marché des Enfants Rouge, which is every bit as packed as L'Wren predicted. And yet, she still somehow manages to get us three seats at the counter with no wait. The three of us sit in the giant market, nestled between a flower stall and a fishmonger, eating ceviche and drinking wine and none of us wanting to say goodbye.

Back in our room, I text Petra, to see if there really might be a chance of seeing her again. She responds right away to say that she is headed to Spain but that she can't stop thinking about the website.

I poked around, through all the fantasies. You have something and I think I can help.

I make a plan to meet her when she's back in Texas and then spend the next hour daydreaming about working with her—the idea is thrilling and maybe a little terrifying. I listen back to some of the interviews recorded over the last few months and sketch in my notebook until I fall asleep.

In the morning, we all wake up early. It's time for the two of them to leave for the airport and I get a pit in my stomach, watching them pack the last of their things and missing our time together already. I kiss them both goodbye, taking in a gust of L'Wren's perfumed air, and they are gone.

I check out of the hotel and take the metro to another part of town, quieter but still beautiful, where I have found a more affordable hotel. At the front desk, a stern-looking Frenchwoman in a paisley apron—seemingly annoyed at how early I've shown up—gives me a metal key with a number. I lug my suitcase up a narrow flight of stairs and hoist it onto the bed just as Jasper texts to say he'll pick me up in an hour.

I unpack some of my things and then I take my pens and notebook to the window. The room is small, just big enough for a bed, a nightstand, and a wooden chair, which I pull up to the window's ledge. I sketch the building across the way, and the young man in front of it, kicking the back wheel of his scooter and cursing in French. I'm still watching him when Jasper approaches, carrying a bouquet of bright pink peonies.

"Are those for me?" I call.

Jasper startles, then finds me in the window, both of us laughing. "Does that mean I'm invited up?"

At the top of the narrow stairway, he hands me the flowers and tells me he can't come in or we'll never leave the room. I tell him that's fine, two of us might not fit in there anyhow.

To start, Jasper takes me to his favorite coffee spot in the third arrondissement, a café in an art gallery, with giant cloud-shaped light fixtures hanging from the ceiling and vintage camera gear for sale on the shelves.

"This looks like a place you've dreamt up." I make a slow turn to study the black-and-white photographs that have been blown up and turned into wallpaper.

"Wait until you see our next spot." He kisses me tenderly and, two coffees in hand, leads me back out the door.

For the next ten minutes we wind through a series of narrow streets, avoiding the crowds as we go. We come to an iron gate and just beyond it, a garden appears as if out of thin air. The sensation is like tripping on a gravel road only to land in a soft bed of feathers. We walk through the garden's square, Jasper taking photos while I admire the climbing roses and overflowing flower beds. We sit on a stone bench and take in the peace and quiet.

"How did you find this place?"

"You don't have to whisper." He chuckles.

"That's just my awestruck voice." I smile. "It's beautiful."

We stay in the square for over an hour, sipping our coffee and sharing a banana cake, until the sun is high in the sky and both of us are flushed and sweaty.

"I don't suppose you have a bathing suit in that purse?"

When I shake my head no, Jasper takes us to a tiny shop selling over-the-top resort wear. We pick out loud, flower-printed suits, and he directs us to the next surprise—a floating swimming pool on the Seine. The line is long and slow-moving, but neither of us minds. When we're let in, Jasper dashes for the roof deck and secures two bright orange sun loungers. We immediately strip down to our bathing suits, both of us stealing glances at each other. I slip out of my sandals and the pool deck burns the bottoms of my feet as we pick our way through the crowd. Jasper jumps in and watches as I ease my torso into the cold water, then submerge myself completely. Underwater, I see Jasper's legs, tanned and strong in his orange-flowered trunks. When I come up for air, he's waiting for me. He pulls me into his arms and kisses me. We don't say anything, just grin at each other, while all around us kids splash and moms scold and serious poolgoers attempt to do laps.

We swim to the edge and rest our elbows in front of us, legs kicking out behind as we watch a tour boat glide by on the river. Jasper's knee brushes against mine and we move closer, desire so close to the surface for us both. We swim a few laps as if to burn off the tension. I'm aware of feeling too old for this life, too old to be so carefree. I thought it was too late for my world to expand, but now that it has, I only want it to expand further. I find Jasper's hand and we float on our backs, squinting up at the sun in the cloudless sky.

With our fingers still pruned, we walk through aisles and aisles of vintage clothing at Jasper's favorite outdoor flea market. I try on a vintage Chanel coat and Jasper buys more denim for his collection. He takes a picture of me sitting in a rattan rocking chair with big square glasses that remind me of my mother. I tell him about her love of rattan and her desperation to be famous as we sip on lemonade.

"Was it all bad?"

"Only sometimes." I don't want to ruin the mood. "Isn't that everyone, though?"

Before we go back to my hotel, Jasper takes me to one more favorite spot, a speakeasy hidden behind a nondescript door I must have passed at least three times already. Inside the windowless bar, Jasper is greeted by name and we're ushered to a booth in the back. Our waiter speaks in rapid French describing complex and well-designed drinks.

"What are you in the mood for?" Jasper asks.

Our waiter is so stern I can't possibly utter the word *margarita*.

"Surprise me," I tell him.

Jasper speaks intently to the waiter for another long moment. I recognize words like *pisco* and *orange bitters* and can hardly believe they are still talking about drinks. Twenty minutes later, I'm presented with a cloudy pink drink in a rocks glass with a papaya spear. It tastes sweet but also like chili pepper and licorice. After two drinks, we drift back to my hotel room so overcome by sun and liquor and the city that as soon as we lie on the small bed we drift off to sleep on top of the blanket, my head on Jasper's chest.

Sometime in the middle of the night, he stirs and wakes me with a kiss. Our bodies find each other, and he enters me with ease. We stay in a dreamlike state as we make love, half asleep but acutely aware of how to please each other. The small bed creaks beneath us, and I realize our eyes are still closed. We've melted into each other, unable to stop. At one point I wonder if it's really happening at all or if we're in a delicious shared fantasy. When I come, a quiet wave rolls through me, a powerful quiver that starts in my chest and runs through my groin.

And then the light is coming through the windows, and Jasper apologizes; he has a meeting today that couldn't be canceled. I should be disappointed, but I'm relieved to have the day to myself. He promises to text later with the plans for the evening party he must attend.

"Can't wait."

I watch from the bed as he pulls on his T-shirt. He leans over me and brushes the hair from my face. "You look so beautiful. You're here . . . I'm just talking because I can't take it in."

I smile and kiss him goodbye. As soon as the door closes, so do my eyes. I fall into a deep sleep.

I wake up at noon and head out into the sunny street, blinking. I make my way across the road and stop at the newsagent for a *Paris Match* and an English paper.

I find a table on the terrace of a wide café near Les Halles. I sit under a canopy of leaves and pull out my newspaper. I order an omelet with a green salad and the waiter is kind and patient with my attempt at French. I try to focus on what I'm reading, but the cells in my skin are softly vibrating with the simple anticipation of seeing Jasper again. Of hearing his voice. My phone buzzes on the table.

There is a surprise for you back at your hotel.

Is it you?

No. I'm later. Meet at my hotel at 6? Then the party.

Perfect.

The surprise is only if you need something to wear of course. It's black tie, at the Dial Building. Wait. Did I just ruin the surprise?

I smile and order another café noisette, which I drink while watching the terrace fill up. A man with a tiny dog is feeding crumbs to a pigeon right under the nose of the waiter, who looks irritated. I pull out a postcard for Emmy and sketch every detail for her. I pay the check and head down the block in no particular direction. Different objects fill my backdrop. A French advertisement, or the green neon cross of the pharmacy, everything is interesting, I'd like to understand everything—the pun in the perfume ad, the conversations in line behind me in the patisserie, the joke the shop clerk makes.

I make my way back to my hotel, where the lady in the paisley apron looks annoyed with me again, this time handing me a large garment bag. I thank her and carry it up the stairs, imagining Jasper and me at the party, the two of us together in a room full of strangers.

Back in the room, I unzip the bag to find three different dresses to choose from, all beautiful—one black and strapless, another metallic brocade, and my favorite one, a red silk dress with a high, delicate neckline. I toss the wardrobe bag onto the bed and notice something heavy at the bottom. It's a white box tied with a green velvet ribbon. Inside are a pair of lacy black underwear and a sheer black bra, both more delicate than anything I've ever worn.

When I get to Jasper's suite, the door is propped open. At first I worry I've entered another part of the hotel, not a private room, it's so spacious. There's a baby grand piano sparkling and untouched in a corner and a fully equipped bar. Speechless, I walk through to the bedroom. Jasper is propped up on the pillow already fully dressed in a black tuxedo, his long legs stretched out in front of him, his face sun-kissed from our afternoon at the pool. He scrabbles in the hotel quilt for a remote and half closes the curtains. He kisses my cheek and after we say hello I slip into the bathroom to fix my hair—it's too much suddenly to be in the room with him. "Jasper," I call through the open door. "Holy crap, this room."

"I know. It was booked for me. It's over-the-top and that's the point, I think."

When I enter the room again, he stands and walks toward me. He looks around, then reaches behind me and pulls an open bottle of champagne from its ice bucket. "It's still cold. What do you think?"

"Why not?"

It feels familiar and new, his lips so full and soft against mine. My desire builds, quick and sharp—have I ever felt like this? I can't possibly have ever felt like this and allowed myself to forget it. I am woozy and almost unsure where I am in the room. I back away and lean against the desk. It digs into my back.

Just then a bell rings.

"Thank god I ordered room service." Jasper laughs and lurches toward the door.

I want to slide down onto the carpet, but I make my way toward the bathroom to look myself in the eye. I run the cold water over my fingers. I bend over the sink and hang my head between my arms.

Jasper raps on the door.

"Come in."

"I brought you more champagne," he says. When I turn to face him, he fingers the strap of my dress, feeling my new lingerie underneath. He lifts the hem of my dress, his fingers on the soft flesh of my thigh, stroking me. With his other hand, he sets the glass on the marble sink, then holds my chin. He locks eyes with me in the mirror. He gently rocks against me. He unfastens my stockings, then fingers the edges of my underwear, tugging them off and dropping them to the floor. He leans against me and closes his eyes. I can feel his heartbeat. "I don't know if you'll want a bite beforehand, but there's some fruit and cheese and some sandwiches." His fingers are light against my skin, his breath on my neck. "Sparkling water." He slips both dress straps from my shoulders, then the straps of my bustier, exposing my nipples. "Oh. Hello." He puts his hand over one of my breasts, his mouth over mine.

I would do anything for more of his breath on my skin, but I feel I shouldn't move—his movements are hypnotizing us both, light and perfect. Rhythmic. He is looking down at my nipple, rolls his thumb softly around it, then he leans down again. "Okay?" he whispers, kissing me lightly on the shoulder, meeting my eye.

"Yes," I manage to say.

He smiles and holds my gaze.

"Maybe you should go without this," he says flatly, unclasping the bra, pulling it up over my head and tossing it on the tiled floor, "and these . . ."—he kicks my underwear aside—"we can come back for them later." He pulls the straps of my dress back over my shoulders, my bare nipples erect against the silk.

He turns me around to face the mirror and grins at our reflection. "Ready when you are."

. . .

The party is filled with pretty people in evening clothes. A woman with a necklace hanging backward down her long, tanned back. A man in tails smoking a long, thin cigar. We slide under the twinkling pendants and through a crush of dark-suited men into a long side room with doors open to a terrace. *Who are these fine people?* I wonder giddily, not wanting to talk to any of them except for Jasper. Women of all ages wear heavy makeup in unusual colors, white paint on their eyelids and dark lips, or fully glittered creams applied up to and across their eyebrows. It's either beautiful or garish, depending on the face, but the overall effect makes this feel more like a masquerade ball than a cocktail party.

The musicians have set up in the middle of the large ceilinged entrance, with terrible acoustics, and so the music floats thinly throughout the party. I'm aware only gradually of Jasper moving us through tightly knotted groups, like bees moving flower to flower, every conversation flowing out of some center I can never find. "This is so I remember to pin down Charlie and force him to tell us what happened to Elvina—" some woman is saying to Jasper. I catch little more than a sentence's worth of any conversation, before the rest is carried off by pure atmosphere, the ambience so thick I doubt anyone is listening to anyone.

We're only halfway up the massive marble staircase that arcs across the center of the room before the champagne starts to get to me. My limbs are made of crumbling powder, and my feet are throbbing. I excuse myself and make my way easily back down—more than half the conversations are in English, but nobody knows me to stop and talk—and I slip outside into the courtyard. My armpits are hot, my neck is hot. I'm thinking only of taking a stroll along the stone balusters, trying to slow my breath. I take in deep gulps of air and still I feel strange and out of control. It's its own climate out here, so dense with greenery, the fragrance completely floral. When I pass a man and a woman smoking and talking near a large flowering plant, she glances up at me. It's too much, even her looking at me, so I pretend to answer a call.

"It's me," I say, some new flame crackling through my voice. I duck my head as a warm gust of air stirs the leaves. "I'm here in the gardens." I couldn't think of anything else to say. I clutch the dead phone to the side of my face and sway, looking at the moon. I could have called Alicia, or L'Wren, but I don't want to be in conversation with anyone, I just want to stare up at the dark purple sky.

I make my way back inside and stand in a clutch of people near the entrance. From there I watch Jasper deep in conversation with someone new. He is electrically present when he looks at you, as if there is nothing and no one in the world as important as you and this conversation. The world around both of you could fall away and it wouldn't distract him. Even now he's up on his toes, just slightly, flexing his fingers, then contracting them into claws circling his hands at the wrist. He catches me staring and smiles. Within seconds, he's back at my side. "One more lap," he says. We make our way quickly through each room of the party before slipping out the door, into his car, and back to the hotel.

"What are you doing?" he says with a familiar smile.

"What do you mean?" I ask innocently. Then I slip my dress off and let it fall to the floor, beside my discarded lingerie. Jasper's eyes ignite with a fire, and the space between us turns thick with desire. He leans back against the bathroom vanity, sipping on his drink.

"A bath can just be a bath," he offers.

"True. We don't need to have sex," I answer as I lower myself into the hot water.

"No, we don't need to," he says with almost no emotion at all.

In response to the challenge, I lift my breasts just above the waterline, my nipples already erect. Jasper smiles and takes a long sip of his drink. "Jesus . . ." His voice is breathy, his eyes not leaving mine, his hand slowly drifting to his pants button.

I trace my fingers along my breast and then down my stomach until they disappear beneath the water. "But I don't want this bath to just be a bath." I tip my head back, the warm water in my hair. I could live here now. In this hotel room with Jasper. "Jasper. We could never leave." My entire life disappears as our eyes fix on each other, a pull so strong it has lasted over a decade.

"I can stay in my corner," he says softly. "I'm happy to just watch."

I lift a wet arm out of the tub and beckon him close. He comes near and I sit up, unbuttoning his pants. I hear the intake of breath as I take his erection in my hand. The sound makes us both smile. I stroke him gently and he bites down on his lip. "You could stay in the corner," I tease. I release him and lower myself into the bath, submerging my entire body. When I emerge, Jasper is holding his thick cock in his hand. Still. Waiting for me to give him permission.

I turn the faucet on and switch to the handheld spray. Then I grab hold of the side of the bath and lift my hips out of the water, pointing the rushing water between my legs, already so full with want. "It feels good." I sigh. The combination of the pressure of the water and Jasper's eyes on me electrifies every inch of my body.

I close my eyes and move the showerhead closer. My nipples tingle. The warm sensation between my legs spreads through me. Jasper is stroking himself now, long and slow. My need for him is almost too much to bear. I need to be filled. I want him everywhere.

"I need you," I whisper.

Jasper strips off his clothes, then steps inside the bath. The water rises as he sits, creating a wave that nearly spills onto the floor. I turn off the sprayer and he pulls me to him, my back against his naked stomach, his erection pulsing against my skin. He kisses my neck. Our shoulders heave at the same time, our breath ragged. Then he tips my head all the way back so he can kiss me deeply, his tongue inside my mouth, his lips hot on mine. His stubble stings my cheek. I let his hands travel up to my breasts and he takes them in his hands, massaging my aching nipples. I reach my hand under the water, between his legs, and play with the head of his cock, circling it with my fingers in teasing strokes. He moans into my neck, low and guttural. And then he takes my wrist in his hand, stopping me.

"Tell me you're mine tonight," he says. The intensity of his voice, as if he could devour me whole, makes me quiver. Instead of answering him, I show him by tipping back to kiss him again, teasing my tongue across his lips, against his teeth, and then plunging it into his mouth.

I come up for air. "Tonight I'm yours. My body is yours." Now I grab his hand, the one holding my wrist beneath the water. I move it between my legs, spreading them completely. His breath is heavy and deep, almost a pant. He reaches behind us and turns the tap back on, grabbing for the sprayer. He lifts my hips above the water, placing the sprayer between my legs with one hand. With the other hand, he rubs the warmest part of me, slipping a finger inside me and massaging my g-spot in small concentric circles.

I let out a low, breathy moan and arch my back higher to give him more access. "Deeper," I beg.

Jasper pushes a second finger deeper inside me, moving in a steady rhythm. My hips rock back and forth above the waterline, my thighs tightening around his hand. The pleasure is unlike anything I've ever felt before—the movement of his fingers as the shower's spray vibrates against me. Jasper is breathing hard into my neck, biting my ear, growing harder and harder against my back.

"Another," I urge him until he opens me wide enough to have three fingers inside. I feel the walls of my vagina pulse against his fingers as he thrusts in and out and my body starts to tense. I'm heading toward my edge, my stomach tight, my hips buckling under the pressure of his touch. The bath is cooler now, the motion of Jasper's fingers thrusting inside me creating small waves that crash over my breasts.

"I'm going to come." It echoes through the marble bathroom, and just saying it out loud gives my body permission. The floodgates open, but before I completely give over, Jasper slips his fingers out of me.

"Wait. I want you to come on top of me. All over me. I want to see you."

Hearing the words coming out of his mouth makes my orgasm build faster. "Hurry."

He quickly gets out of the tub and lies down on the marble floor; I quickly follow. I straddle his upper torso and lift my hips toward his face. I can't move fast enough. My orgasm is impossible to slow down, so I spread myself open, inches away from his mouth, and move my fingers in and out. I cannot stop. The pleasure is so intense and fast-moving that I'm no longer in control.

"Come all over me. I want to see it."

"Put your fingers back inside me."

Fuck, it's so good. I keep moving against his fingers until I feel an intense rush. I am coming. For a moment there's a relief but before I can catch my breath the pressure builds again, even stronger. I cry out for a release.

"Oh god." At the sound of his voice, I come again onto Jasper's chest. He opens his mouth and pulls me to it, hoping to taste me.

"It's so fucking good," he moans between my thighs.

As he sucks on me, the pressure builds again—this time my toes curl as the orgasm rolls through me harder and harder until I explode, every nerve on fire with ecstasy. I break all at once.

"Fuck . . . fuck . . ." Jasper says as his body tightens from his own orgasm. He pulls me to his chest and comes onto my stomach. He shudders against me. We are both completely spent.

I slide off him, lying beside him, trying to cool off and catch my breath, my legs quivering.

"You're a fucking goddess. Promise me you'll do that every day we're together. I'm serious. Promise me."

"I don't know if I can ever do that again. It's the first time it's happened to me." I laugh, still in disbelief that my body reacted the way it did.

"Good. Don't do it with anyone else."

"I won't. Just you." My eyelids feel suddenly very heavy and I let them close, trying to quiet the small part of me that has already started to think about making the trip home.

PART THREE

Dallas, Texas

Chapter Nine

—

As soon as Oliver opens the front door, Emmy comes running. "Mommy!"

I scoop her into my arms, all limbs and wet hair, still damp from Oliver's pool. "I missed you so much!" It's only been a week, but I swear she grew taller at camp.

"Did you bring me a present?"

"Emmy!" Oliver laughs. "At least thirty seconds of love before you expose your true self?"

He looks different too. His hair is a little longer and his face is unshaven.

"Hmm, well. . . ." I pretend to search my bag long and hard for a gift. "I might have something in here? Let's see . . ."

Emmy's face lights up when I pull out three gifts: a pair of soft pink puppy-dog pajamas wrapped in fancy tissue paper and tied with a silk ribbon, which she pretends to be interested in; a glittery rhinestone-encrusted jewelry box in the shape of the Eiffel Tower, which she sets aside; and a book on tigers, which she opens immediately.

She sits on the floor of Oliver's living room and flips through the pictures while also asking, "No candy?"

"Check the jewelry box."

There she finds bright pink strawberry-shaped gummies. Her eyes widen. "Thank you! Can we play hide-and-seek?"

"Ems, your mom had a long trip." Oliver offers me a drink.

"Sure."

Emmy goes back to her book, tracing her finger across the illustrations and sounding out the French, while I follow Oliver to the kitchen. "Your place is looking nice." He's hung more art since I was last here. A series of framed photographs of vintage boom boxes from the eighties.

"I had to fight against the decor stereotype with everything I had."

"Which one?"

"Sad Divorced Dad."

At the word *divorced* we both flinch. "Hmmm. Let me check your freezer." I open it to find it's packed full of frozen fruit and espresso beans, no sad TV dinners in sight. "You passed."

He smiles, a full, even smile. He squeezes lemon into my iced tea and hands me the tall, thin glass. He rocks back on his heels, his back against the fridge, and we sip our tea, standing as far apart as possible in his bachelor kitchen. I was so excited to get home and back to Emmy, but being here now, I feel homesick—for Alicia and L'Wren, for Paris, for my little hotel room, and for Jasper and the electric feeling of being near him.

"How was the trip?"

Emmy interrupts, coming to stand directly between us. "Now

can we play hide-and-seek?" She takes me by the hand and down the hall, toward Oliver's bedroom.

"Do you have time?" Oliver calls after us.

"One quick game and then we'll take off."

"You guys hide together," Emmy instructs.

"We don't hide together, silly." Oliver has followed us into his room. For a moment, I wonder if he's afraid of what I'll find. But we're separated—what's there to hide?

"Your dad and I should pick different spots so you have lots of places to look."

"No. I want you both in here. I'll count." Emmy closes the bedroom door. The two of us scan for options. The room is small; there are no curtains to hide behind, and Oliver's bed has built-in drawers underneath. That leaves the closet. It's barely big enough for both of us, cramped and dark. I sit on my heels while Oliver squeezes in next to me and shuts the door. The bare skin of his arm brushes against mine. Something sharp is digging into my right hip. I adjust myself. "I was sitting on a boot."

He laughs and shifts so that we are facing each other, opening up a few more inches of space. "Better, right? Tell me about Paris."

"Oh. She's coming—"

Oliver's bedroom door opens. We listen as Emmy's footsteps creak on the floor outside the closet. And then retreat, out of his room and down the hall.

"I'm confused," Oliver whispers. "She *chose* the hiding place?"

"Em-*my!*" I call loudly.

Nothing.

"I'm worried about her short-term memory."

"Oliver. We'll give it one more minute."

Oliver shifts again, but there's no more relief to be found in such a small space.

"Did you get nice weather in Paris?"

"Beautiful. Sunny every day."

"Diana. . . ."

I bury my face in my knees. I know what's coming. "I don't want to talk about the picture."

"What picture?"

I look up into his face, arranged to be perfectly neutral. "Thank you."

We sit in the quiet. The silence between us has changed. It feels unfamiliar. Charged, even. My eyes have adjusted to the dark and I can make out Oliver's face more clearly. I can see the sweep of his long lashes. "What is it?" he asks.

"Nothing. Jet lag." I shake my head and then call, "Emmy?"

Quiet. And then . . . in the afternoon stillness, I make out the faint sounds of electronica music and a familiar voice asking kids to *like and subscribe*. I press my ear against the back wall of Oliver's closet. "That's Mr. Beast! She's watching YouTube. Your daughter's stranded us in a closet for extra screen time."

Oliver grins. "Well played, Emmy. Well played."

"I guess she forfeits? Good timing. My feet are asleep."

Oliver watches me stand, then finally lifts himself, his body even closer to me now.

"Do you want to see the house I'm flipping? It's near the trampoline park. We could take Emmy and wear her out and then I'll drive you both home."

"I don't know. I seriously smell. I should probably get home and shower."

He leans in to take a sniff. "You'll blend right in at the trampoline park."

I get a second wind, chasing Emmy through the trampoline park, until we all decide to call it. It's only a five-minute drive from there to the flip.

Oliver pulls into the stone driveway and Emmy skips toward the back to pick dandelions in the overgrown yard.

"She's my little helper. And by helper, I mean she promises not to complain while I work, but then she asks to leave every three minutes."

At the front of the house, Oliver has cleared all the weeds and dead leaves, along with three dying trees, and is planting rows and rows of colorful zinnias. "My favorite," I say, but he doesn't meet my eyes.

"So you can actually see the front of the house now," he tells me, "which has massive curbside appeal."

He unlocks the front door and it's impossible not to see the house's charm—it's exactly what a young couple would want. A storybook first home.

"I found these old windows in a junkyard. It took me a week to sand and stain them, but they came out pretty well."

He shows me the kitchen, still in pieces, but with new cupboards and an island made from an old draper's table.

"It's really lovely, Oliver. You've done all this yourself?"

"I've got a guy helping with the electrical. And two guys coming to do the insulation. But everything else, yeah. I still need to seal the floors. Something matte, I think. And the faucets haven't come in yet, so I'm waiting on those."

He's radiating happiness like he did when we first met, when he would stay up late into the night, sketching furniture designs and planning future travel. *We should go to Stockholm,* he would say. *Look at this architecture. Maybe I'll build us a hotel. Or Lisbon. We can bring back tile for our kitchen. Or maybe we stay in Italy? Just long enough to learn how to speak Italian and make a good pizza.*

"I was nervous to show you. I'm glad you like it."

Out the kitchen window, we see Emmy lying on her back in the grass. "I think we did a good job of wearing her out."

. . .

At home, Emmy and I eat cheddar omelets and sweet potato fries and we take turns reading her new tiger book with terrible French accents. I've already showered, but as soon as Emmy is asleep, I run myself a bath. I slip in and the water is so hot, my skin blushes a deep scarlet. I force myself to stay here until the water cools, and when it does, I slowly sink underwater, my entire body submerged. I imagine the young couple who will want to buy Oliver's house. I picture them the way Oliver and I used to be—not only dreaming about the future but believing that the *feeling* you were reaching for was right around the corner—the permanent sensation of being exactly where you're supposed to be, a confidence and contentment that drowns out any doubt. Oliver should put a claw-foot tub in the new house, for the couple. An extralarge one so they both can fit. The water should be hot, so she can stay in for as long as she likes.

Chapter Ten

—

Home in my own bed, I get a fitful night's sleep. I'm dressed and ready for work by five A.M. I wait for Emmy to wake, then drop her at her grandparents. When I get to my office, I find a giant gift basket, overflowing with long, oversize strips of beef jerky, dried deer meat, and a bottle of warm Chardonnay. The card attached reads:

> *Thanks for putting in a good word with Petra.—Allen*

I spend the morning at my desk, but it only takes me a couple hours to catch up. My favorite email is from Petra:

I guess by now you've heard I'm officially keeping my money with the old shriveled dicks! See you around the office. xoxoxo

By the time Liam texts asking if I'm free for lunch, I'm starving.

He offers to come by and pick me up: *There's someone I want you to meet.*

Is this a setup? I'm not dating any of your friends.

Gross. And no—I'm still scarred from watching you flirt at the mall. Remember?? I sure do.

"Hey," Liam says as I climb into his car. "Ugh. What's that smell?"

"It's a thank-you." I plop the gift basket on his lap. He wrinkles his nose but picks through the free stuff anyway.

"Where are we going?"

"Not far."

I roll down my window and we drive across town, picking up burgers along the way. We eat in his car, and he hurries us through the meal. He drives fast with the stereo as loud as it goes and we hum along, until Liam pulls up to a massive ivy-covered brick house.

"Are you moving out of L'Wren's basement?"

"And forfeit a lifetime supply of free La Croix and my dad's low-grade disdain? Bite your tongue."

As we get closer to the front door, a smile spreads across his face.

"Liam. Tell me."

"We have a new employee. For the site."

"You hired someone?"

"Sort of. An intern. This is her place."

"Liam . . ."

But he's already ringing the doorbell and soon a petite blond woman appears. Her eyes are warm but she doesn't smile, and it's hard at first to guess her age—she's dressed much older than her features suggest. She runs a sensibly manicured hand down her calf-length beige skirt. Her hair is held in place with bobby pins and hairspray.

"Diana, this is Kirby." Liam beams. "She looks like a Fox News anchor but that's just her vibe."

"Liam," I scold.

"It's fine." Kirby's smile is small and polite. "It's actually true that I've never met an Ann Taylor Loft I didn't love." She holds out her hand. "It's a pleasure to meet you, Diana. Come in."

Liam and I follow her into her home, which is neat and tidy and looks like it belongs to someone who always uses a coaster.

"Kirby was a music major at SMU."

"Woodwinds, originally."

"She plays the clarinet. Like a beast."

"Then I switched to composition. I thought for a minute I might like music therapy but . . ." She pulls a face that suggests we should know exactly how crazy an idea that would have been. Liam laughs like he gets it.

"And now she's looking to get into sound design. So I sent her a few of the Dirty Diana interviews."

I'm less surprised that Liam has gone rogue and more preoccupied by trying to get a read on Kirby. "So you've listened to the interviews?"

"I spent time on two of them so far." Her expression is completely neutral.

When she doesn't follow up with what she thought, I ask, "Where are you from?"

"Highland Park, born and bred, but my parents are originally from River Oaks in Houston. I was meant to be a Kinkaid girl, but my mom ended up homeschooling me. And by 'mom' I mean the myriad of paid academics she hired to teach-slash-raise me."

"See?" Liam digs his elbow into my ribs. "She can totally afford to intern."

If it's an insult, Kirby doesn't register it as one. She leads us farther into her house and into a small room, soundproofed, with two large computer monitors and several keyboards. "Liam thought maybe I could play you something. If that's okay?"

"Sure."

She hands me a pair of professional-looking headphones and gestures to the love seat. Liam and I sit. "I'm interested in sound design, obviously, but I'm also interested in collaboration, in the intersection of art and commerce, and in entrepreneurial work, specifically, and witnessing something built from nothing."

When she speaks, it's deliberate and confident, almost like a party trick, never an *um* or an *uh*. She makes me want to sit up straighter. "We're not really a proper business," I tell her.

Kirby shrugs. "Not yet."

"I had this idea"—Liam jumps in—"while you were away, for a way to elevate some of the interviews, something new to try. And I met with Kirby and she took my idea and made it way better."

"We can listen?" she suggests.

I put on the headphones. At first it's strange to hear my own voice—but it's so immediately obvious that Kirby's made the experience of listening to the interviews more pleasurable. I listen closely, trying to dissect exactly what she's done to make the sound so much more intimate, but whatever it is, it's subtle. The audio has been cleaned up and she's added a few tones as transitions. It gives the interviews polish. When I look up, Kirby is watching me—for the first time she does look exactly her age, her eyes wide and expectant. When I tell her how much I love what she's done and how I can't wait to hear more, her shoulders relax. And when Liam catches her eye, she breaks into a grin.

Outside, I shield my eyes. The sun is bright and between the jet lag and being in Kirby's small, soundproofed room, I have the most disoriented feeling—suddenly I'm unsure how long I've been at lunch and away from the office. I walk to Liam's car in a daze.

He opens my door for me. "She's a nice fit, right?"

I nod and close the door, my head swimming, thinking about what Kirby rattled off so easily about collaboration and how she's taken what we've been working on and made it better. "My friend Petra offered us some space in her suite of offices. She has an entire empty floor that she never uses. Maybe we should think about it. A place for all of us to work together sometimes."

"So you like Kirby?"

"Liam, I think *you* like Kirby."

"Whaaaat?" He blushes. "True. But it's totally one-sided. The Dirty Diana HR department has nothing to sweat."

Chapter Eleven

—

The next week passes in a blur of long hours at work, swimming at the community pool, and hot, sticky nights catching fireflies in the backyard with Emmy.

Jasper is in Berlin, seven hours ahead, and calls every few days, usually as I'm getting into bed. He likes me to guess: "Am I just coming home or just waking up?" I ask him to describe the night he just had or the day ahead of him, and he peppers me with questions about Emmy and what I've been thinking and making. We don't talk about when we'll see each other next, but it hangs around heavily in the background.

When we hang up, the texts roll in:

Thinking about you.

Remember that time in Marfa? When we pulled over on the side of the empty road?

God, I adore you. Where are you right now?

. . .

Some mornings, I drive the long way to work, slowing down as I pass Oliver's renovation, sometimes catching a glimpse of him working outdoors. For the past couple days, he's been constructing the front steps. At first I found it inspiring, watching him toil away at something he loves. But with each passing day, I worry more and more about the money he's spending. Since he moved out our bills have been steadily mounting—there's the reality of our mortgage, combined with rent on a second place. Today as I drive past, there's a large stack of paving stones out front near the zinnias, and this stack looks different from the stones that have been laid so far. I have the sinking feeling he's going to rip out the ones he just laid and begin again.

At the end of the week, Liam, Kirby, and I move our things into Petra's empty offices, in a three-story white brick building on the edge of town. Petra's PR firm is run from the top floor and we'll be just below. No one is there on the weekend when we arrive, but she has the security guard meet us out front and show us up to the second floor. It's a pretty space, bright and light, with thick-planked oak floors and a big window that takes up most of one wall and looks out over the street. I move in Oliver's old drafting table and some canvases and set myself up against the window's bright light. Kirby takes a small office for herself, then she and Liam get to work soundproofing a recording space for me. Liam takes an empty desk for himself, right up front near the kitchen. He brings Kirby coffee and heats up lunch for them both.

Once we've unpacked, I find a mostly empty notebook and sit on the blue love seat that Petra has lent us. I listen back to an interview and re-create the woman from memory. I start by sketching her most distinctive features—full lips, soft wavy hair, sharp nose, the slope of her neck.

When I take off my headphones, I hear Liam and Kirby laughing. Kirby is perched on his desk, our site pulled up on Liam's monitor.

"What's so funny?" I stand and stretch, needing a break from drawing.

"We're reading the comments."

"Where are the comments?"

"Have you ever visited a website, Diana? Scroll down." He sits me in his chair and leans over my shoulder. He smells like coffee and peppermints, which I imagine he pops just for Kirby. "Some are clearly from the ghost of Newt Gingrich but most of them are really cool. Look . . ." He scans the page, reading as he goes:

Love the honesty of these interviews. Why aren't there more?

YES. Going back to listen again.

Paintings are very pretty. Are they for sale?

"Liam . . . I can see you scrolling past all the mean ones."

The next day, I drop off Emmy at Oliver's for the long weekend. He's taking her to his mother's annual Fourth of July BBQ and I'm *thrilled* not to be invited to spend the afternoon in the judgmental swim of Vivian and Allen.

"I think my mom wants to set me up with her friend's divorced daughter." Oliver sighs. "Someone from her DAR chapter, of course."

It's no surprise that Vivian has moved on so quickly from me, but it still stings. I change the subject. "How's the house coming?"

"A few hiccups but getting there."

When I don't respond right away, looking at a point somewhere over Oliver's right shoulder, he snaps, "Please don't, Diana. Not right now."

"What?"

"What *what*?"

"Oliver, I didn't say anything."

"I know what you're thinking."

"You're the one overreacting," I say, annoyed that he can still read my mind.

We slip into old patterns so easily, arguing like children. Emmy stands nearby, focused on her colorful stack of friendship bracelets but absorbing the tension between us.

Oliver lowers his voice. "You're nervous about the money and how long it's taking. Why can't you just say what you mean?"

Anger whips through me. "You're giving me communication advice? Like how you overcommunicated about spending our money."

"At least I'm trying."

"What does that mean?"

Oliver puffs up his cheeks, then slowly exhales. "I don't want to do this. Not right now."

"Of course you don't. You never do." I paste on a smile and grit my teeth. "Have fun with the socialite. Maybe she can give us a loan!"

My anger dissipates on the drive home—the heat of my outrage cooled by a frosty coat of shame for being so childish and allowing my buttons to be so easily pushed. I remind myself of today's victory: not having to stand around Vivian's backyard eating mayo-soaked food that's been baking too long in the sun. That counts for something, right? The twinge of triumph is short-lived. As I near home, I remember the yawn of three days alone in the house. I had thought that after Paris it would feel different, that I wouldn't mind being home alone and I would sleep fine once again. It's still not true—the house without Oliver and Emmy feels strange. When I picture the empty rooms, my body tenses.

But as I turn into my driveway, Jasper is waiting for me.

Chapter Twelve

—

Jasper sits on my front steps, his face tilted up to the sun. When he sees me, he breaks into a smile. I can't help myself. I slip directly into his lap and wrap my arms around his neck. He looks sexy and disheveled and my heart races. I hadn't realized how much I've missed him.

He hugs me against his chest, then lifts my hair and kisses the back of my neck. I pull back to face him and lift his shades, falling into the pool of his deep brown eyes. "What are you doing here?"

"We're going away." He smiles. "I need an assistant. A big out-of-town job. I thought you might be able to help me out."

"Ha ha." We both remember the early morning in Santa Fe a million years ago when I found Jasper freezing and pacing out front of my work, desperate for me to help him on a photo shoot. Fifteen years later, I feel the same butterflies in my stomach.

"It'll be better than Marfa, I promise." He stands and takes one of my hands lightly in his.

"You're serious? You just got here."

"I got *here* to come get *you*. Come on, pack your bag." He pulls me to my feet. "Two nights. I'll have you back bright and early Monday."

I take a step away, as if lost in consideration and playing hard to get. He closes the gap immediately, his hands cupping my face. He kisses me softly. And I whisper into his mouth, "Emmy's away until Tuesday."

"Three nights." He grins. "Even better."

The front seat of Jasper's rented Bronco swallows us up. We drive for hours, stopping for BBQ and a quick swim at a secret swimming hole he knows about. Then we're back in the truck, driving across the rolling landscape of Texas hill country, past Whataburgers and detention centers and off-ramps for towns that slip by too quickly. We keep the AC off and the windows down, the summer air warm against our skin.

We stop in Fredericksburg for dinner. Jasper and I walk the main street, hand in hand, taking in the antique shops and historic buildings, quietly wondering exactly what the other is thinking. When we stop at a window display of especially terrifying antique ceramic clowns, I keep my eyes straight ahead. But I can feel him watching me. I turn and smile, and when our eyes meet an ache goes through me, a longing for him to touch me. We share a strawberry ice cream at an old soda fountain, passing it back and forth, licking the dripping ice cream before it melts onto our hands.

"Where next?" I picture a tiny bed-and-breakfast with lace doilies and a resident cat.

"It's a secret," Jasper says, and we hop back into the truck.

Just outside of Fredericksburg, Jasper turns onto a dirt road and drives slowly down a gentle hill with a campsite at the bottom. My heart sinks a little at the thought of no indoor plumbing for three days and mosquitoes snacking on us all night. But we keep driving until we come to a crystal-blue lake, surrounded by six A-frame treehouses, perched high above the ground.

"This is where we're staying?"

"Pick whichever one you like."

I choose immediately—a slender treehouse with its door painted blue—and climb the steep stairs to the top.

"A buddy of mine built these when he retired, to tempt his grand-kids into visiting more. Now he's given up on them and just lends them to friends. Wait till you see the view."

We put our bags down and take a tour. Off the bedroom, high in the trees, is a porch strung with fairy lights, overlooking the lake. I peer over the railing while Jasper makes himself comfortable in a yellow-and-white-striped hammock. He stretches out and folds his hands behind his head, but even in a hammock, he doesn't look totally relaxed. He keeps one leg flung over the side, his foot on the ground, ready to spring into action at a moment's notice.

It's quiet, except for the sound of chirping frogs calling to one another. Jasper gets up and moves closer. "Can I kiss you?"

"Yes."

Jasper rests his forehead against mine and exhales. "Finally. We're together." He kisses me deeply, his tongue inside my mouth, and it all begins. We can't hold back another second. Before we realize what is happening, he's unbuttoning my dress and my fingers are sliding down his chest to his belt buckle.

"I missed you," I tell him.

"Let's not go so long again."

I nod, both of us pushing thoughts like *But how? How could we possibly live our lives so far apart and see more of each other?* from our feverish minds.

He scoops me up in his arms and carries me inside. He lays me down on the bed. I stretch my arms up above my head, inviting his exploration. The mattress dips as he kneels over me, straddling my hips. Slowly, he leans down and kisses me everywhere—my breasts, my shoulders, my neck.

"You're even more beautiful than the last time I saw you," he says.

"It wasn't *so* long ago." His kisses stir my craving—I'm desperate to feel him inside me. The feeling of him pushing into me, filling me up, so familiar and still so new.

I run my hands along the bottom hem of his shirt and then tug, asking silently for him to take it off. He discards it immediately, pulling his shirt up over his head. I run my fingers down his naked arms. Outside, the summer sun has dipped completely and the only light in the room is from a bedside lamp, glowing soft and orange.

"Take it off," I say.

"Which part?"

"All of it."

I undress, too, and slip beneath the crisp sheets. And then we find each other, our naked bodies pressed close. "God, I've missed you." I reach for him, drawing him closer until finally he's on top of me. He smiles and kisses me softly. In response, I lift my hips, begging to feel him inside me. He doesn't make me wait. He plunges into me and pleasure crashes over us. Immediate and unwavering. His lips are on my neck and his breath is warm. The stubble on his chin is just the right amount of rough. His erection is hard and thick and every movement is bringing me to the brink of orgasm. I let go and sink into the pleasure. I bat away the tiny, annoying voice reminding me just how temporary this bliss is. That it will depart, alongside Jasper, for London or Paris at a moment's notice, without me. I drown it out. I focus on my body. The sensation of Jasper moving inside me. He tilts his pelvis forward, knowing the exact spot to touch me. Gliding against me, over and over again. When he speaks, his voice is raspy. "This is all for me." It's laced with more awe than greed.

I smile into the thick muscles of his shoulder. "All for you."

As he moves, I tighten my legs around him. We alternate fucking and making love. We look into each other's eyes and move together, slowly and deliberately, only to hurriedly grasp for every piece of each other, a tangle of hungry, sweaty limbs. A pleasure deep inside me begins to furiously multiply. It's happening so quickly, but I can't slow it down. "I'm going to come," I gasp. I fall into a full-body shudder as the most delicious sensation races through me, on the edge of orgasm.

"God, you're beautiful." The sound of his voice makes me tremble. I press into him and he keeps riding me, his jaw tense, pushing in and out of me as tiny white lights burst around me.

"I'm so close," I say.

And with one last push, I'm over the edge. I cry out in ecstasy and he stills, his mouth open, and I feel him pulse as he comes inside me.

Still hard, even after he climaxes, Jasper rolls over onto his back. We lie side by side, trying to catch our breath.

"Let's stay here forever," he tells me and we both laugh, letting ourselves imagine living in this bubble.

When the sky has gone completely dark, we wrap ourselves in a blanket and sit out on the patio. We listen to the frogs and pass a cold bottle of beer between us.

"How can sex be this good?" he asks.

I grin. "It's great. It's always been great between us and it still is."

"'Great'?" he repeats. "Hmm. 'Great' feels like one above 'fine.'" He takes a long drink from the bottle. "I want *incredible.*"

"Well. We have the whole weekend."

"True." He kisses me and I can tell he is nowhere near satiated. I feel a familiar ache between my legs as his lips press against mine. I'm relieved when he says, "But we probably shouldn't waste any time."

I slip the blanket off our shoulders and spread it beneath us. He watches me as I lie back on my elbows. "Come here." I look up at him, framed by the night sky, then wrap my arms around his neck, pulling him closer. Jasper's erection grows as he closes the space between us and presses against my thigh. His skin is perfectly silky and soft to the touch. I stroke the plump head of his erection. I bring it closer to my mouth, brushing him against my lips. Then my face. I softly kiss his inner thighs, making my way up, licking and sucking his skin.

"Diana . . ."

My tongue rolls over the swollen head of his cock, and I suck it softly while running my fingertips up and down. I take Jasper farther inside me and my lips reach the base of his shaft, then I slowly suck my way back up to the tip. "Oh god," he moans. "That's it . . ."

I pause and pull away to look up at him. He smiles at me in disbelief, his breath becoming more ragged. As my tongue slides back down his shaft, he gently thrusts forward inside my mouth. I take him all in and Jasper runs his fingers through my hair. I wrap my fingers around him, gripping him tightly, then slide my hand up and down, sucking the head of his penis, squeezing my hand around him. Jasper moves his hips.

"Diana." He's close. "I want to be inside you."

I want him inside me too. Desperately. I take him from my mouth. I straddle him, pressing my hands against his chest. I resist the urge to move too quickly and take him inside me completely. I slow things down. I circle my hips, allowing the tip of his penis barely inside me, then lowering down onto him until he fills me up. Again and again. We do this for what feels like hours, neither of us wanting to stop.

When he can't hold on much longer, he says, "Let me see you." I move off of him, stretching my body alongside his. Our shoulders touch, both of us hot and breathless and so comfortable in our nakedness and our longing. He brushes his fingers against my cheek. "You're so beautiful, I can't take it."

Hungry for an even deeper sensation, I turn onto my stomach. I smile at him in invitation. He grins and moves closer. He's on top of me now, his smooth, muscular chest pressed against the curves of my back. I lift my hips, asking him in. "You want this?" His voice is dripping with desire.

"Yes." My body relaxes as he enters me. "I want you everywhere."
I grip the blanket beneath us, my hands in tight fists, and we move like this, lost in ecstasy, until neither of us can wait another second. He sinks into me and the pleasure is more than either one of us can bear. Jasper's body contracts and we come together, Jasper moaning into the nape of my neck.

It's late morning, we're in bed drinking coffee. My body is sore and still shaky. Jasper has left the treehouse once to buy us coffee and donuts. I haven't left at all.

"Where would you want to live?" He rests his chin against my naked stomach, his stubble tickling my bare skin. "If you could live anywhere."

"I don't know. I loved Paris. Maybe Brazil. Tokyo."

"I want to take you to Mallorca. For at least six months."

"I can't just pick up and go anywhere . . ."

"Why?"

"I have a daughter. And a life in Dallas."

"We'll bring her. She can learn Spanish."

"Maybe."

"Have you been painting? Do you have any photos?"

"A few. I've been playing around with more Dirty Diana interviews."

I take out my phone and notice two new voicemails from Petra. I swipe them away, with a mental note to call her as soon as I'm home. Then I pull up the site and Jasper and I page through it together. I show him a finished painting and then one that I am still working on.

"Diana."

"Yes?"

"I'm finding it really hard to concentrate."

He takes my coffee and places it on the table beside us and then pulls my hips down on the bed, quick and hard. My phone falls from the bed to the floor as he climbs on top of me.

"What's one of your fantasies? Do I know?"

"No."

"Tell me."

"What's yours?"

"Nice try. Tell me."

"Maybe my fantasy is this. Treehouse and all." I turn my cheek and our lips touch, both of us tired but still craving each other.

"My fantasy is keeping you in my pocket." He rolls onto me, his forearms framing my face. "Total access."

"So, imprisoning me?"

"Mmm. In a consensual, fun way. Like even right now. In this room. You feel like mine."

"I am." I kiss him deeply, then flip us over, pinning his arms over his head. "And you're mine."

"Okay," he whispers between kisses. "And we live in Mallorca. We all speak Spanish. What else?"

"What will you do in Spain?"

"Stay still. Be happy and totally static. For once."

"You? Still?"

"You calm me. Being near you. I could sleep for a hundred hours tonight."

"You never sleep."

"I do now. With you." He pulls me into him, my head resting on his chest. "Watch me. Watch me close my eyes and never move again."

Chapter Thirteen

O liver's gaze flits to my unpacked suitcase, still sitting by the front door. "Were you away?"

"In Fredericksburg." Both our tones are light, if a little cool. We're feeling each other out, to see if we're still in a fight.

"What's in Fredericksburg? Wait." He holds up his hands. "Never mind. It really is none of my business."

"How was the socialite?"

"Her name is Katherine. Nice, actually. Surprisingly nice."

"Good." It doesn't feel good, but I say it anyway.

"She's not really a socialite."

"What is she?"

"A baroness." This melts the tension between us for real and we both smile.

"Your mom must be levitating." I watch the way Oliver's mouth can't help but turn up into a grin, the slight blush in his cheeks. He really likes Katherine. I'm happy for him; he's met someone nice. And still, my skin burns with jealousy. The same skin that still smells like sex and Jasper.

Before he turns to leave, Oliver says, "Diana?"

"Yeah."

"I was thinking. What if we went back to therapy?"

"Really?" For weeks after he moved out I had suggested this to him, again and again, before finally giving up.

"I know. I never thought I would say those words either. But I was thinking it might help this process? I don't want us to fight. Or worse, not fight and just be weird and tense around Emmy. Maybe there are tips to make it easier? Especially if we're both, you know, dating again." He shoves his hands in his pockets and looks up at me from under his thick lashes. "Or maybe I just stop asking you about Fredericksburg?"

His expression is soft, a look I recognize as *I'm trying.* "It's a good idea," I say. "To make sure we're doing this right."

"Right."

"Especially with a new school year coming up," I say.

"Yeah, we should go back to therapy." He rocks back on his heels. "For Emmy."

Hours after I put Emmy to bed, I lie awake thinking about Jasper. He's decided to stay in Texas for an extra week. "I have meetings I can take. People I can see. Especially you." Then my mind skips to Katherine, trying to imagine what she looks like. I think of Oliver and the last time he was here in this bed, how we almost had sex before he kissed me goodbye through a blanket. The memory makes my cheeks burn with embarrassment.

I kick off my covers and make my way quietly downstairs. I want to feel okay again in this house, even without Oliver here. To fall asleep easily and wake up refreshed after long, restful hours. Instead I stare up at the ceiling and fall asleep for what feels like minutes before my alarm goes off. Then I drag myself out of bed and into work like a zombie.

In the kitchen, I make myself a cup of tea that promises sleep and open my laptop. I pull up the site and scroll right to the comments.

Totally lost myself! Thank you!

Empowering!

Can't with the raspy voice. Someone get Diana a lozenge!

Where's the video? Why so cheap?

I read through all the good and bad until I come to a block of comments from the same person—a series of comments that goes on for pages. I keep scrolling, discovering someone has written an entire fantasy in a series of fifty-three comments. The first one simply reads:

I want to fuck my therapist.

But the following comments are long and take up pages:

I've lied and told him I'm a sex addict. But it's not true. I don't even have real vices anymore. The only thing I'm actually addicted to these days are chocolate-covered pretzels and thinking about fucking my therapist.

His name is Henry and he's a very kind, sensible man in his late 40s, who collects rare coins. I told him I was dating all the time, which also isn't true. I told him I was worried I was having too much sex. Another lie. So he gave me the following rules to live by:

No oral sex on the first date. No penetration on the first date. Only after the fifth date can I sleep with someone. If I make it that far. No masturbating in front of my date. I know it seems obvious but it's helpful to have it in writing, I tell him. Kissing is fine on the third date. No going over to my dates' houses after ten p.m. when they text me "you up?" Sex does not give me power over anyone. Sex does not make me more worthy. I have a problem, I explain. I need to follow the rules.

I've never told him I want to have sex with him. I guess if he's halfway decent at his job, he's figured it out by now. And he is so much better than the others. I needed someone stern. A therapist that has a real perspective. The rules are there to help me.

In my fantasy, I call Henry at three A.M. and tell him it's an emergency. I need to see him now. It can't wait. He sleepily agrees and tells me to meet him in his office in fifteen minutes. I hear him apologizing to his wife in the background, she's not happy that he's leaving.

Henry is waiting in his office when I arrive. He's wearing a white button-down shirt and gray trousers. A rumpled blazer and wire-rimmed glasses. He's handsome in a bumbling Hugh Grant kind of way. I smile when I see he dressed in his usual uniform. I'm still in my nightgown. Freshly showered, but still.

When I sit down on the striped couch opposite him, he immediately takes out his leather-bound notebook and looks down. He typically doesn't look me in the eye during our sessions, focused mainly on his notes.

With his head down, he tells me this is the last time he can meet me this late. Just like he told me last time I fantasized about him. But it sounded urgent, he says. So.

It's a dream I had.

A dream? Not a nightmare? he asks.

No. It was a good dream. I was falling. From the top of the building. But I knew I would never hit the ground.

He scribbles this down.

I go on. I was naked in the dream. And the air was so warm. And the fall excited me. It didn't scare me, I tell him.

It doesn't have to scare you to be a nightmare. Do you ever hit the ground?

No. It was frustrating. It went on so long without ever landing. Just falling.

How are you feeling now?

Horny.

Henry doesn't react. Just writes it down.

Actually, the dream makes me want to touch myself.

Henry looks up in surprise. Then immediately back down at his notes.

That is not appropriate in this office, he says.

It won't take me long. I'm already wet from the dream.

We've talked about this. There's a slight panic in his voice.

You don't even have to watch, Henry. Look. Just close your eyes and I'll tell you when to open. I pull my underwear to the side and spread my legs, facing him. I want him to look. I need him to look.

What should I use, Henry? My fingers?

Please. You know this is wrong. Enough of this.

I'll use my fingers then. I slip two inside me and start to perform. Oh god, Henry. Oh god. This feels good.

Please stop. I'm asking you to stop.

You don't really want that, do you?

Yes. He's flustered. I can't do this.

Fine. But this isn't working for me. I need more. I slide my fingers out of my pussy, my legs still spread. See?

This isn't how I run my sessions.

I'll leave now. On one condition. Can I see it?

See what?

Your cock.

Henry blushes.

No one would find out, I promise.

He studies me for a minute and then sighs. You've developed a strategy for when you feel this way. When you feel the need to dominate. Remember the rules.

Show me your cock. And then I'll go.

Would you like some water? he says, growing increasingly uncomfortable.

No. I want to see your cock. I can tell it's hard. I can see it stretching the fabric of your pants.

Henry crosses his legs, turning away from me. I show you and then you leave?

I promise.

Henry checks the door to make sure it's locked, then unzips his pants and pulls out his cock. It's even better than I imagined. Smooth and thick. Pulsing with excitement.

There. You've seen it.

Please let me suck it.

Absolutely not.

But you're so hard. I think you want to feel what it's like inside my mouth. What if I just sit on your lap? Is that okay?

He doesn't answer.

Henry.

I have an early client.

I'll be quick.

He leans back in his chair and I climb on top of him. My legs straddle his so if he decides to let me go further I'll be ready.

We're so close we might as well, I whisper.

I kiss him and he opens his lips slightly, just enough so that I can slide my tongue into his mouth. He moans softly. He's starting to break. He won't be able to say no soon.

I could lose my license, he whispers. Please.

Then why is your dick so hard? I'm going to stick it in and you say no if you want me to stop.

I guide him into me and he moans louder and louder. Mmm . . . mmmmm. But he isn't saying no.

Please.

Please yes or please no?

But his eyes only widen as I sit back and take his entire cock inside me. He groans out loud and slowly starts to rub my thighs as if coming alive. He can't hold back anymore. He wants this. I kiss him again and raise myself all the way up to the swollen head of his cock, then slowly, very slowly, lower myself back onto him.

Oh god.

Oh shit.

And finally, he kisses me back. Everywhere. My neck, my lips, my tits. He cups my ass cheeks and I ride him hard.

This isn't good for you, he says. We shouldn't . . .

It's too late.

We fuck like that for what feels like hours. Henry lifts me up and down, varying his speed and his depth until his thrusting becomes more urgent and he's rock-hard inside me.

I'm close. I'm so close.

I ride his shaft faster and faster. Up and down until we're both seeing stars.

God, I'm close.

Then I whisper in his ear, I love the feel of your cock inside me. I love that you did this. I could live with you inside me.

Henry throws his head back in bliss, his dick starting to spasm inside me.

Say it. Tell me how much you like it. That you've always wanted it. I smash my hips into his pelvis, securing him deep inside me, and tighten my walls around him.

Henry's eyes roll back, his mouth open, panting.

Don't stop, he says.

Tell me.

You're the fuck of my life! he shouts, and I feel him come deep inside me. A surge of power washes over me as he climaxes. I'm completely satisfied.

I slide off him and open the door to his office before he can stop him. His wife is outside. She takes one look at us and screams. She runs for the exit. His patients are also in the waiting room. Looking at Henry in disgust.

Henry calls to his wife but she doesn't answer. He scrambles and pulls up his pants. Then he looks at me, scared. What do I do? Tell me what to do. He pleads with me. He looks broken. Permanently broken.

And I realize I've just lost the best therapist I've ever had.

I don't know, I tell him. I can't help you.

But you'll stay with me. We'll be together, won't we . . .

No, Henry, I say. That would be against the rules.

Chapter Fourteen

—

Oliver and I sit in the waiting room outside Miriam's office. "Thank you," he whispers over the burbling fountain, "for doing this."

"Of course." Petra is calling me again but I send it to voicemail, realizing I completely forgot to call her back after the long weekend. "Thanks for squeezing it in so early." We're both being overly polite, which is my secret hope for the entire hour. In preparation for our first session, I downloaded a new family calendar app and packed a day planner and colored pens in my purse. I've let myself daydream about what it could feel like to get to a place where I drop Emmy at Oliver's and I don't feel a sinking, panicky dread as I walk back to my car like I've left something important behind.

"I don't know what it will be," Oliver says, "but maybe Miriam will help with some of the lingering stuff that still needs to get sorted."

"Lingering stuff?" My heart drops. This doesn't sound like color-coded schedules.

The door to the inner office opens and Miriam greets us.

We take our familiar spots on opposite ends of the couch—the same exact spots we sat and fought in months ago, just before Oliver moved out. I half expect them to still be warm.

"It's wonderful to see you again." Miriam settles into her chair and crosses her ankles. "Oliver explained to me when he made the appointment that you're in the middle of a separation?"

"Yes. We're hoping for some tips on how to do it right," I say. "If there is a right way. For Emmy."

"Of course. It's very admirable to still be committed to having the healthiest relationship possible. But since it's been a while, bring me up to speed. Let's have both of you state how you feel, sitting here today, next to each other."

Of course it was magical thinking to hope we could come to therapy and avoid talking about feelings. And yet . . . I can feel the part of me that just wanted to talk calendars and parenting tips slowly deflate, leaving the raw part of me exposed—the part that has to deal with divorcing Oliver.

Beside me, Oliver exhales as if his bubble has been punctured too. "I feel sad. And also like an asshole. Who made a lot of mistakes."

I look up from my lap, surprised. This couch is the scene of blame and recrimination, not apologies.

Then he says, "I think we both made a lot of mistakes. Diana too."

There it is. I sit up straighter, crossing my legs and perching myself on the edge of the couch.

"Okay, but let's stay on you for a minute, Oliver."

Thank you, Miriam.

Oliver shifts uncomfortably. "I've been unhappy for so long and a part of me blamed Diana for that unhappiness. And that wasn't fair."

Miriam talks as she scribbles notes. "And what do you think about today, when you think about the source of your unhappiness?"

"I don't know. I didn't understand it for so long. It was just something I felt in my body. And then one day . . ." Oliver's voice hitches. He rubs his face, the way he does when he's tired. "One day I was walking into the office and my chest started pounding. And then it got tight, so tight that I couldn't catch a good breath. I stumbled back to my car and I was gulping like a sad, bigmouthed fish and I thought I was having a heart attack. I was sweating, a cold sweat, just like they say happens. I couldn't move. And it was so pathetic, crouching alone in the office parking lot, clutching on to the bumper of my car, thinking I might die. And I kept thinking, *Please don't let Diana find me like this.*"

"Oliver, when was this? You never told me—"

Oliver shakes his head. "It wasn't a heart attack. It was a panic attack."

"That must have been very scary." Miriam's voice is calm.

"It was eye-opening. I knew I had to do something. It's like I had to blow up the life I was living to find a path to get out of it."

"So you knew you needed to change, but you weren't sure how."

"Why didn't you tell me any of this?"

"I wanted to quit that job for so many years. Quit working for my father. But I kept thinking I could still impress him. Like I would crack the code one day and win him over. I know, it's ridiculous. You know him, he doesn't change his opinion of anyone."

"Oliver, he's proud of you . . ." I picture Oliver in Allen's office, visible through the glass, Allen picking on him for who knows what, Oliver's shoulders slumped.

"Oliver, what do you hear when Diana says that?"

"I appreciate her being nice. But there's no truth in it."

"And what else?"

"It's confusing. With Emmy, she could impress me by whistling. She doesn't even have to do it correctly. She can try and I'll be impressed. Like, genuinely impressed. I didn't understand how my father couldn't give me something. The bare minimum."

"He loves you, Oliver."

"He doesn't. He scares me. And that's not love."

"Of course he does."

"Please, stop. It was hard enough to come to this place."

"What place?"

Oliver pauses before he speaks. "My dad just doesn't like me. Nothing I do will ever be enough for him."

My heart sinks. I've spent years watching Oliver try to please his father. I would take little acknowledgments and turn them into big wins just so Oliver wouldn't one day say this sentence out loud.

I try to imagine the thousands of tiny but painful admissions it took for Oliver to get to this. I had encouraged their relationship. I never once took Oliver's side. Maybe because it was too sad to believe.

"I chased a love that wasn't there for so long. And it broke me. I saw myself how he saw me."

"How does your father see you?" Miriam pushes.

"As a failure. A disappointment. And I became that. At work. In my marriage. And as hard as I tried to impress my father, it didn't happen. So I stopped. I stopped trying. I quit that job and I feel better. It's not that simple, of course, but I was miserable. And I kept thinking, how is that attractive? I hate my job. I hate going to the office. I was a shell of a person, yet I expected Diana to shower me with attention."

"What is this bringing up for you, Diana?"

I wasn't expecting any of this. "Sorry. I'm just taking it all in. Oliver . . . Sorry," I apologize again, trying to find my footing. "I thought we were here to talk about Emmy and how to help her through this . . ."

"Yes, of course," Miriam interrupts. "But don't you think this would help—to understand why your marriage is ending?"

I turn to Oliver and see he's already looking at me, his eyes hopeful and soft. He wants to understand. I thought I had understood.

"Diana?" They are both waiting for me to answer. So I do something I wasn't expecting I'd ever do in her office: I tell the truth.

"Yes. I would also like to understand."

Back at work, I run into Allen in the kitchen. "Jesus Christ, Diana, are you okay?"

"I'm fine. Having a little insomnia." *Also, I was just bawling in my car after therapy with your son.*

"Well. Let me buy you a cup of coffee." He fills my mug from the office coffeepot, his favorite joke.

Before I can politely thank him, his current sycophant, Doug, swans in. "Sir. I had a copy made of the Petra portfolio."

My ears perk up at Petra's name.

"Diana, Petra's invited you to this meeting." Allen is picking over a box of free donuts that look like they've been sitting out for hours. He pops a powdered sugar donut hole in his mouth, seeming to swallow without chewing. "Let's go."

"Now?"

"Now."

Petra is already seated at the conference room table with sparkling water and a relaxed grin. "Diana, I tried calling and calling."

"I'm so sorry, Petra. I've been buried." I take a seat across from her and smooth my hair.

Are you okay? she mouths.

I nod as Allen cuts in.

"Petra, I know I speak for all of us—"

"You do like to do that, Allen," Petra jabs and we all laugh politely, Allen loudest of all.

"Hard not to speak for all of us when we're all so excited to see you today and discuss ideas."

"Doesn't that sound magical? Well, actually, as it turns out, I've got something potentially very exciting."

"Wonderful," Allen says. "One of the real estate opportunities we showed you? Can't go wrong with land."

"No. It's more . . . tech."

"Tech? I didn't realize that was on the list. Doug, is that something we talked about?" I watch Doug silently panic and leaf through the paperwork, as if he might find something new in the deck.

"Not entirely tech," Petra says. "It's more of an enterprise, really. I want to be in the female wellness space, in a bigger way."

"Recipes, fitness, that kind of thing?"

"Not really. It's a website. For women."

The blood drains from my face.

"Sure, okay. There's a plethora of promising start-ups we can research—"

"Don't bother. I've done the research."

Petra catches my eye and smiles and I feel my heart pound.

"It's an erotic website for women."

Doug stifles a laugh with a cough. Allen just looks confused. "I'm sorry. I'm not following."

Doug leans into Allen. "I think she means porn."

"Yes, I understand that, thank you. I'm trying to understand the investment appeal."

"Petra's joking." I feel my shirt sticking to my back. "Obviously."

"I'm not joking, Diana. I thought you'd understand that."

"You want to invest in a pornographic website?"

"I think 'erotica' would be a better word for it. But I've never been one for labels."

I flip through the portfolio in front of us, the one that Doug has spent weeks preparing—and I feel my face burn red-hot. "I think you may be better served by a more trusted investment opportunity."

After a long pause during which I can feel her eyes on me she says, "I don't agree. I like this for me. Mitch would have too."

"So you've seen this . . . erotic website, Diana?" Allen asks.

"There's nothing really to see," Petra says. "*Yet*. That's why this is such a good opportunity. Right now, it's just an idea. And as is, maybe it'll circulate to a small group of friends, maybe get a small following and a little word of mouth. And then what? All that hard work and it just evaporates into the ether of an overcrowded marketplace? Another good idea lost? From what I can tell, there's no real strategy in place for a proper launch, and no real capital in place for any marketing and PR spend. It would be a lift, for sure. But I'm up for it."

"Petra!" I catch up to her as she slips into her car. When she turns, she's beaming. It's as if what happened in the conference room was something we had rehearsed. "I know. *I know.* This is going to be very fun."

"No, Petra." I shake my head. "Allen is my father-in-law."

"Diana, no shit. Don't you get it? You won't have to work at this frat house anymore. We can work together, and I can give you a salary. But really, you'll be your own boss."

"You should have talked to me first." I squeeze my fists, feeling the sharpness of my own nails.

"You never called me back." She puts a hand on my shoulder.

"I'm sorry. I meant to."

"What's going on? What's wrong?"

"Nothing. I'm fine, Petra. I've just been busy and I'm not sleeping great but I'll figure it out, just a little insomnia and Oliver and I— Petra, I know you want to help, but I'm fine."

"Diana, you have a real knack for laying your emotions at the feet of the wrong people. You let your father-in-law get away with everything and you're pissed at me for no good reason. I'm here to help and you can't see it."

"I've worked here a long time."

"I get it, Diana. I understand. But I'm not sure you do."

. . .

I take a walk around the office park, avoiding Allen. I stop in the shade of my favorite maple and dial Alicia's number. She picks up after four rings and whispers, "Hey, everything okay?"

"Oh shit, sorry, are you in class?"

"Don't worry, I'm out in the hall. We're screening the freshman shorts today and they all think they've made *Nosferatu* and I have no idea what the fuck any of them are about."

"Get back to it. I love you."

"I love you too. Call L'Wren."

"Why? What's wrong?"

"Call her."

Maybe she heard I've been working with Liam. I feel terrible, I should have told L'Wren all about the Dirty Diana site by now. I meant to tell her in Paris, of course, and then didn't. I meant to tell her so many times, but I just wanted it to get on its feet first, before I told too many people about it, before I felt judged by them. I dial her number and plan out what to say while it rings. But I don't have a chance to speak before L'Wren blurts, "I'm getting a divorce!"

"What?"

"I know, Diana. It's all so horrible. I know exactly how you felt. You can't understand it until you're actually going through it, can you?"

"Wait. Catch me up. When did this happen?"

"Even though I knew it was heading in this direction, my heart needed time to catch up, I guess. And then our therapist practically encouraged it. The truth is Kevin wasn't happy either. He didn't say it out loud, but you can't work that much and not be running from something. God, I feel like such an idiot and such a failure. But even idiots can find a way to stay together. Why can't we?"

"Because it's not the right fit, for either of you. Maybe it used to be and now it's not."

"We took vows. That should mean something. Especially in Texas."

"I'm so sorry, L'Wren."

"Diana?" I hear her sniffle. "I know it's a terrible club to belong to, but I'm glad we're in it together."

"I'm not officially divorced yet."

"Well, neither am I, but you know . . . Our ships are both pointed to that port."

"How about if I come over?"

"No. It's okay. Kevin is still here. He's so blasé about the whole thing. Like this was all part of our journey."

"I'm sorry," I say again.

"But what did I want? For him to beg? I mean, no, not really. But maybe a little? I feel like one of his business failings. He's just so matter-of-fact about it all. Which I guess is for the best."

I think about L'Wren for the rest of the morning, sending her texts from my desk, reminding her she's not alone and that it gets easier. But my own lie takes me by the throat—she is alone, and some days I feel so lost I can hardly breathe. Then I remember I do have someone I can call—Jasper. Someone who runs me baths and orders me room service in five-star hotels.

When Jasper picks up I say, "Hey. It's been a day."

"It's eleven A.M.," he says with humor in his voice. "Tell me everything."

"It's messy and complicated . . ." And the details are giving me a dull, throbbing headache. "I just want to see you."

"Let's meet at the hotel. I've got a coffee with a collector that the gallery owner is making me say hello to. I can make it quick and be back there in an hour."

"Yeah?"

"Yeah. I added your name to my room so you can get a key from the front desk. Diana? I'm really glad you called."

On the way to the hotel, Petra texts me.

Is now a bad time to tell you about the Dirty Diana vibrator prototype I've had made?

She's hard to stay mad at. *Funny. And yes, in case you're not joking, it's a bad time. I'm sorry about earlier.*

Don't worry about it. I'm not writing to convince you. You should move things at your pace.

Thank you.

But I do think you should get a few marketing materials together. A proper headshot—that you can use or not use.

Okay. I just need to come clean to a few people first.

Come clean? Now that's a great tagline.

When I get to Jasper's room, the first thing I notice is a new bag of hair products on the bathroom counter. An expensive oil. A creamy texturizer and a mousse. Does he really use three different products every morning? Make it four—there's an antifrizz spray on the counter. I walk to the minifridge but all the sodas are missing, replaced by a neat row of green juices. The first three are marked *Prep.* I unscrew the top of one and it smells like broccoli and cumin. The rolling wheels of a maid's cart pass by the hallway and I dart outside and ask the housekeeper for water. She graciously gives me three of the tiniest bottles of water I have ever seen. I drink them all like shots. When Jasper's not there by twelve thirty, I open my laptop to do some work. At one thirty, he sends me a text:

Sorry, everything here is taking longer than I'd hoped. Order some lunch. And don't leave!

I tell him not to worry, I'm on my third glass of Prep.

Woman! he jokes. *Leave my vanity alone!*

At two forty-five, he texts again.

Sorry. So many unexpected drop-bys at our meeting and all long-winded talkers. Trying to escape asap.

I tell him again not to worry, even though I feel a fluttery panic at remembering this part of us. In Santa Fe, Jasper was constantly agreeing to meet me at a party, only to decide later he didn't want to go. Or he'd show up and be the center of the fun, then slip away early, expecting we'd find each other later. I felt tethered to him by an invisible rope that he could tug when he felt like it and let it go completely slack other times. And instead of walking away, I tried to figure out how to make wherever I was the only place he'd want to be. I thought I could hold the rope in my hands and then we'd be in balance—and it was only at the end that I realized he wasn't even playing the same game as I was. I spent months after our breakup trying to decide if he had ever really made the promises I was convinced he had broken. And now? He's in a hotel for a couple more days and then he's off again. I panic at the thought of feeling that tug, a hard jerk on the rope that sends me falling, slipping backward.

A knock on the door and my hope returns—that quickly. But it's not Jasper. A masseuse dressed in clean white scrubs enters the room with her massage table and smiles warmly. "You must be Diana?"

"Yes."

"I'm Sybil. Jasper asked me to take very good care of you."

An hour later I'm so blissed out on Sybil's table that even when I try to conjure up my deepest worries—about Jasper, about Oliver, about Emmy—they flit away, covered in sweet-smelling almond oil and massaged out of me. Getting upset in the office, the rivers of anger I feel for Allen—all of it washes away. No one can predict the future. Certainly Jasper and I are different people than we were in Santa Fe. Why do I need all the answers? As Sybil runs her fingers along my temples, I take calming breaths, inhaling deeply and letting myself drift off to sleep.

I wake up in a plush hotel robe underneath fifteen-hundred-thread-count sheets surrounded by lofty down pillows. By the door sits a new suitcase surrounded by shopping bags. Jasper bought a bigger bag. And more clothes. He extended his trip.

"Hello, gorgeous," he says, sitting on the bed beside me.

"How long have I been sleeping?"

"An hour? Maybe more. Good massage?"

"Life-changing."

Jasper's already eaten, but he's ordered me dinner. After a shower, I wrap myself back in the hotel robe and he watches me eat. "I like the idea of taking care of you tonight. Like I would if we were together. When you have a hard day and I'm at home waiting for you. If this was real."

I dip into the pasta and take one delicious, mouthwatering bite. He ordered me some of everything, including a strawberry milkshake for dessert.

"Don't you agree? This would be nice?"

"For us to be real?" I want to say *I do, I want us to be real.* But it's hard to say that while in a four-thousand-dollar-a-night suite with meals delivered to our room and a maid to clean up our messes. "Sure. Let's practice."

He smiles. "Hi, honey, how was your day?"

I think about unfurling my laundry list of what went wrong in my day, but I don't want to bring any of it into our bubble. "I just really wanted to see you. To see if you could make me feel better."

"I think I can. Definitely."

"Prove it," I say as I take a sip of my milkshake.

Jasper studies me for a moment, his gaze making my whole body flush with heat. He stands and takes the milkshake from me, then pushes me back on the bed. My robe falls partially open and he tugs on the tie, exposing me completely. He stands over me, watching me, then with his knee, he spreads my legs.

"What are you doing?"

"Proving it." He holds the milkshake close to my chest, tipping the glass.

"Jasper . . ."

He tips the glass again, slowly dripping the milkshake onto my breasts. I gasp as the icy cold liquid hits my nipples. And then the warmth of his mouth as he licks the ice cream from my skin, his tongue slowly circling my nipples, over and over again. I arch my back, moaning in pleasure at the sensation, cold then hot. He licks my chest completely clean. But he's not done. He sits up again and this time he pours it down my stomach, making a slow trail from my ribs, circling my belly button, and then down to my hips. I suck in my breath as he parts my legs even farther and pours the icy cold liquid onto me, spilling into the folds of me. I struggle to catch my breath. Jasper's head is between my legs, his hands squeezing the soft flesh of my thighs, licking the milkshake clean from my body. Long, slow strokes with his tongue starting at the top of my clit all the way down, then he plunges his tongue deep inside me.

"God, this tastes good."

"Here . . ." I lead his hand closer to me. "There's more . . ."

Jasper smiles and takes me in his mouth again, massaging me softly with his tongue in slow, agonizing circles.

"That's it," I say. "Right there."

I lift my hips toward him, grabbing for his hair and pulling. I want to be all over him. My moans fill the room.

"I need you inside me," I gasp. Then I find my breath and call it out, louder. "Now." I turn over on all fours. He holds me by the hips and then brushes himself against me, teasing me from behind, moving back and forth but not entering me. I feel his erection pressing, then plunging, into me. "Yes, yes." My legs start to tremble. I want it so badly. That his body belongs in mine. I'm full and ready to climax but not wanting to. I want to savor it. I want him inside me over and over again.

His hips thrust against me and I gasp. His body drapes over me, his cheek against my back. I arch farther to give him even more access. It doesn't feel like enough. I want more of him. I need more of him inside me.

As if hearing my thoughts out loud, Jasper moves faster. It's so heightened. So unbelievably raw.

"Is this what you wanted?"

"Yes." All of you.

Jasper draws his speed out, easing in and out of me as I moan in ecstasy. I grip the bed frame and circle my hips, controlling the movement. But the pressure is too much. It builds inside me and I hold on tighter until both of us cry out, letting go.

We lie beside each other, my head on his shoulder. Jasper kisses me hard and we steady our breath.

"Can you stay longer?" I ask.

"Another few days—then a quick trip to New York—then back to Dallas."

But all I hear is "back to Dallas."

Chapter Fifteen

—

Jasper's week in New York turns into two weeks. Then before he can get back to Dallas, he needs to go last-minute to Oslo. Returning to Dallas is up in the air.

"You should come with me," he says over the phone from New York. "Meet me here. We can spend a night in the city, then fly out together."

"It sounds incredible. But I can't sneak away again."

"Who said anything about sneaking? Can't you just tell Oliver you're going on vacation? You must have vacation days at work?"

It still sounds strange to me—Oliver's name on his lips. "Next time. We'll make it happen."

I don't get into the details of the school year starting and the list of things I have to do between now and the end of the week: register Emmy for fall soccer, answer an endless stream of email at work, volunteer at L'Wren's cat adoption fair, and track down something, *anything*, that will help me stay asleep. I've tried an entire shelf of CVS supplements and nothing helps.

After I drop Emmy off for her first day, I sneak away to spend a rainy morning alone in the studio, no distractions, just the pounding rain against the windows. Within minutes of sitting down to paint, my phone chimes with a news alert, followed by a text from my mother-in-law wanting to know Emmy's holiday schedule, then a calendar reminder from work. I shut off my phone completely and sink into the love seat. I flip through my sketchbook of half-finished drawings. For the first hour, I skip around, adding detail to one woman's eyes or fixing the way another woman's hair falls across her face, then spend the next several minutes on a new sketch of a woman, her back to me. I stop to stretch and check my phone. I turn it on to find a string of missed texts from L'Wren:

I did it.

I kissed Arthur.

Omg.

Call me.

You know by "kissed" I mean much more.

We had sex.

Before I can dial her number, I get a new text from Alicia:

Made it back from the silent retreat!! Thank god. Thinking this might have been something to say no and not yes to? Still processing. Have barely spoken in FIVE DAYS. Must UNLOAD. You around?

Followed immediately by more texts from L'Wren:

It was amazing, btw.

Where are you?!

Call me!

Which one should I call first? My phone is silent for seconds before Oliver texts:

What's Emmy's teacher's last name? I'm trying to put money in her eWallet for the bookfair but she keeps saying Ms. Trish. Is Trish a last name?

Another text from Alicia:

WAIT. WHAT. L'Wren slept with Catman? Amazing. She's blowing up my phone. Should we conference you in? Call us.

Then Liam:

Bad news. Something's wrong with the audio on the last interview. We may need to re-record. You around?

Oliver again, this time with a photo attached:

Does this rash look like a "whatever" rash or like a "I should be concerned" rash? It's all over Emmy's big toe.

I imagine chucking my phone across the room and the satisfying crack of it hitting the floor. I respond to Oliver first, Alicia next, then Liam, and finally call L'Wren, listening intently while returning to my drawing of the woman's back. I sketch her neck, then her face in profile so that she's looking over her shoulder. With her head turned this way she reveals herself to me: I carefully sketch the outline of my own nose, the shape of my ear, the curl of my lips.

"There was nothing wrong with our marriage," Oliver says. I tune back in, trying to ground myself on Miriam's couch. "There was something wrong with *us*."

"Do you agree with that, Diana?"

"Everyone is working on something," I offer.

"Not just something. Not just resolutions at New Year's, like drinking more water and being kinder. We had real, unaddressed trauma."

Miriam scribbles faster than usual. "Can you give an example, Oliver?"

"Yeah." He clears his throat and sits straighter. "Like sex."

My pulse quickens—I feel betrayed by my body. By my own duplicity. My dishonesty. How can I be asking other women about their desire when I can't handle talking about sex in here? With Oliver.

"See? You don't even want to talk about it."

It must be all over my face. "Luckily we don't have to. We're getting a divorce."

"You faked orgasms."

"What?"

"You faked having orgasms when we had sex and I knew."

"How did you know?"

"I just knew."

"That's not true."

"It didn't feel like you were having an orgasm. Your body. Nothing was changing. It felt like you were performing for me. Trying to get me to go faster."

I look at a spot just over Miriam's shoulder, my eyes scanning her bookshelves, disappointed to find more purple geodes and tiny clocks than books.

"Were you faking orgasms?"

Who am I to judge Miriam and her decor? I'm the biggest fraud in the room. I imagine how many others have come through here, sat on this couch, and honestly spilled their secrets and shared their grief. I fight the urge to lie again. "Yes."

"Why?"

"I don't know."

"You do."

"I thought it would make you feel better."

"It didn't."

It didn't make me feel better either. My own pleasure was drifting further and further away from me every time I lied. My needs, unmet. My husband feeling empty beside me and not knowing why.

"Diana! How are you?" Katherine exclaims, holding her arms out for a hug. It's only the third time we've met but it's impossible not to hug her back. And not just out of reflex, not just because someone is unfurling to meet you—life actually feels brighter in her arms. With her wide smile and candy almond eyes, she exudes the kind of optimism that draws you close. It's easy to see why Oliver has fallen hard and fast.

"Hi, Katherine. Nice to see you."

"You look gorgeous as usual." She leans against Oliver's doorframe, easy and natural. "Where do you get your facials?"

"A Bioré pore strip?"

"Ha! You are so funny. Emmy cracks me up too. She's got your sense of humor. I'm thinking of taking the girls to the zoo next weekend—did Oliver clear that with you?"

Add "thoughtfulness" to the growing list of reasons she's wonderful. Vivian must be over the moon. "That sounds great. Thanks."

"Let me go get Emmy. She and Taylor have been playing grocery store all morning—but all they sell are parrots and Band-Aids." Katherine also comes with a built-in playdate for Emmy—her six-year-old daughter, Taylor, a miniversion of her mother, who is just as kind.

"No problem. Tell them I'll take a parrot to go!" I try to match her effortless sunniness but it comes off like I'm trying too hard.

Katherine disappears as Oliver appears, holding Emmy's gymnastics bag and stuffies.

"Water bottle and outfit inside," Oliver says. "I was going to tell her she doesn't have to wear her underwear with her leotard because it bunches up in this weird way and none of the other girls do, but when I said it out loud I was convinced it should come from you."

"Got it." When he hands me the bag, my hand brushes his and a warmth runs through me, a sensation I'm not expecting.

"You okay?"

"Oh, yeah," I recover. "I'm not sleeping great."

"You haven't had Emmy. I would have thought you had gotten tons of sl—" He stops. "Oh. Right. I fell right into that one, didn't I?"

"It's not that." What is it then? I don't want to admit I don't sleep in the house without him there. "Work is busy . . ."

When I can't come up with a better excuse, he changes the subject for us. "How's L'Wren?"

"Better."

"I really thought they were going to make it."

"You did?"

"Well, I didn't think they were going to get divorced. What happened?"

"I think they fell out of love."

Oliver bites at the inside of his cheek. "I should reach out to Kevin. It's been too long. Obviously."

"Yeah. I bet he would appreciate that."

I have the urge to give Oliver a hug—a giant Katherine-like hug—and tell him how hard this all is. That even though I can hear Emmy happily playing with Katherine's daughter in the background, it's still hard. This isn't how it was meant to go. On a sunny, cloudless day, we declared to a room full of people that our love would always be there. And then it wasn't. We set it down for a minute—wasn't it just a minute?—and when we turned back, it wasn't where we'd left it. We could argue over who put it where and tell each other *that's not where it goes*. But what difference would it make? Arguing over where you set a thing never makes it reappear.

Chapter Sixteen

—

"This feels like high school again." L'Wren applies an extra coat of mascara to my lashes. "God. It's delicious. I'm nervous. Excited. I've got all the feels. Anything could happen tonight!"

"I like seeing you this way," I say into my bathroom mirror.

"Thank god we are doing this whole divorce thing together. I wouldn't have been able to do any of it if not for you. And I'm dying to get to know Jasper."

"I think you're going to like him." I haven't seen Jasper for weeks and he's only in town for two nights, but he promised he doesn't mind spending one of them on a double date.

"And you are going to love Arthur. At least I hope you do. God, what if you don't? Don't tell me unless you do, okay?"

"I'm sure I'm going to love him."

"How do I look?" L'Wren does a spin in her pale pink dress.

"Gorgeous and effortless."

"Are the heels trying too hard? Too high? I haven't cared what I looked like in ages." She smooths her dress and adds another gold bangle to her stack. "That's not true. I always care. But you know what I mean."

"You do and you don't. And you're stunning."

We arrive at the restaurant, a small vegan café that Arthur has raved about. L'Wren grabs my elbow and squeezes. "Ohmigod. He's here. Isn't he handsome?"

"Where?"

"Curlyish hair, with the dark blazer and glasses. And the cute butt."

Arthur spots us and smiles.

"We had sex on his lunch hour. I can't get enough of him. Don't worry. I showered."

He's not at all what I imagined. When L'Wren was with Kevin they always felt slightly imbalanced. She was charismatic and beautiful and he was brusque and exacting. Arthur's eyes light up at the sight of L'Wren and his smile is gentle and warm. I can feel immediately that there is nowhere else Arthur would rather be than close to L'Wren.

"Diana. This is Arthur. Arthur, Diana."

"Nice to meet you." Arthur takes my hand in both of his, then kisses my cheek, a soothing twang in his voice. I panic suddenly that Jasper will be late. Or not show at all. But then I feel his arms around my waist, holding me tightly. He shakes everyone's hand, and I watch L'Wren warm to his charm.

At the table, he listens intently to L'Wren recount meeting Arthur for the first time.

"How new are we talking? For you two?" Jasper asks, genuinely invested in their love story.

"Officially?" Arthur asks. "Not long at all. But we've known each other for years. L'Wren's brought more cats into my office than any rescue I work with. Can I share your bill from last year?"

"Absolutely not."

"Let's just say L'Wren could've bought herself a second home at the beach."

She swats his shoulder.

"A modest one." He laughs. "Not directly on the water."

Jasper laughs too. "You obviously have a very big heart, L'Wren."

"Only when it comes to animals." L'Wren smiles.

The waitress interrupts to rattle off the specials. Instead of balking, Jasper announces, "Vegan meatballs made of sunflower seeds and cashews sound interesting. What are we thinking, friends?"

"I hope this place is okay? It's hard to be a meat-loving vet," Arthur says. "Like a pyromaniac fireman."

"I feel so much better since I cut out the red meat," L'Wren admits.

"It's killing us all, really. And I really need you around. You know, to keep the lights on at my clinic . . ."

L'Wren punches him playfully. "You're the best vet in Dallas. You'd be fine without my caravan of flea-ridden misfits. I do miss a P. Terry's cheeseburger." She sighs. "I can't help it."

"You could do meat Mondays?"

"Maybe."

They kiss again, this time in blissful agreement. I catch Jasper smiling into his menu.

"Sorry. We're nauseating. Arthur's got me on a health kick. I love it and I hate it."

"And you've got me on a diet of pickleball and pedicures. So we're even."

They lean in for a kiss yet again and it's like a nature show about cute furry animals that crossed a desert to finally find each other. Jasper squeezes my hand under the table but it feels slightly forced, as if we're trying to catch up to them. But we don't need to, I tell myself. We have years of undeniable chemistry. We're happy too.

"So. Jasper. What was Diana like in Santa Fe? I want to know everything."

"She was . . . hmm . . ."

I see the twinkle in his eye and shake my head.

"What? You were . . . adventurous. But not as confident. Not as mature as you are now."

"Ugh, god, Jasper, never call a woman 'mature,'" L'Wren teases. "No, I know what you mean. Diana is so grounded. I've always loved that about her. But I sure would love to meet Santa Fe Diana too. She sounds like a party."

Jasper laughs. "She was an incredible artist. *Is* an incredible artist. Have you seen her paintings?"

I hear Jasper's phone ring in his pocket and he politely excuses himself from the table without an explanation. I watch him through the restaurant's front window, nervously pacing, his phone pressed to his ear.

"Emergency?" L'Wren asks.

"I'm not sure," I say, worried he's being rude.

"I like him," she adds. "He's very handsome."

"He is that," I reply, wishing her compliment were sturdier. Based on something other than his looks.

After I've moved a wheatgerm pancake around my plate in an effort to have it appear eaten, Jasper returns to the table with a wild look in his eye.

"The book sold."

"What book?" L'Wren asks.

"It's a large-format photography book I've been working on. I showed a few images to a publisher last week, not thinking anything would ever come of it, and she just made an offer. Now I've got to get to Iceland to shoot the cover. And some additional landscapes I want to include . . ." I can see his wheels turning, his mind already somewhere over Reykjavík.

"You actually sold a book?" Arthur asks in awe.

"Who wants to go to Iceland?" Jasper jokes.

"Oh, me!" L'Wren lifts her glass.

"How long will you be there?" I know I should start with "congratulations" but I can't seem to find the words.

"Don't know yet. Can't be too long."

I feel L'Wren's eyes on me and I force a smile. She fills in the silence for me. "To Jasper!" We toast.

After dinner, we head to Jasper's friend's party in the Cedars district.

"Thank god I didn't bring a hostess gift. Could you imagine?" L'Wren eyes the very attractive and mostly younger crowd. "Me walking in with a candle?" She touches Jasper's shoulder and whispers, "Are we too old to be here?"

"No! Renee is amazing. They've worked at the gallery for ages. And they love old people!"

L'Wren smiles and we move deeper inside, weaving our way across the room. The loft is packed wall to wall, bodies pushed close together. People all around us dance without inhibition and the energy is contagious.

We find a place to sit and Jasper and Arthur offer to get us drinks.

"I'll have a skinny marg!" L'Wren turns to me, eyes wide. "This is wild!"

"It's fun, right?"

"Are you sad that Jasper is leaving?"

"No. A little? It's great. The book. It's such a great thing."

"It's okay to be disappointed."

"It's just how we are. As a couple." I try to be casual. "This is what we look like."

L'Wren nods, unconvinced, and Arthur hands her a drink.

"No skinny margs," he shouts over the music. "But they did have a Crown and Coke."

"I haven't had Crown anything since . . . high school maybe?"

"Cheers." Jasper holds up his beer. "To new friends."

As we take our first sips, Arthur gets a call from his answering service and apologizes, he's needed at the clinic right away. L'Wren's eyes sparkle, watching him in action. "I'll drive you!"

Jasper and I stand at the edge of the party, watching the dance floor. He brings me into his arms and holds me tightly. "I like your friends."

"Jasper!" A petite woman with an elegant gray bob kisses Jasper on both cheeks. "I'm *shocked* you came."

"Of course I did." He turns to me and adds, "This is Irena. She runs the Bluestone gallery."

"You must be Diana," she offers, but doesn't extend her hand.

"It's nice to meet you."

Her eyes flit to Jasper. "Do you want to circulate tonight?"

He scans the party. "Not really."

"Good. Neither do I. The Dallas art scene can be so cringe. But then, so can I." She says it so matter-of-factly it's charming. "What do you do, Diana?"

"Taxes," I answer at the same time Jasper says, "She's an artist."

Irena's head tilts.

"In my free time," I say.

She doesn't press for details, instead keeping her focus on Jasper. "If you don't want to check in with Joseph and his sycophants, then I will."

"Thank you."

"They're on ayahuasca anyhow so I'm sure they won't even re-member who they did or didn't meet. I told them to stay close to the bathroom."

Jasper and I watch her squeeze between a couple dancing close and disappear into the crowd. "I think I like her?"

"That's the great mystery of Irena. You'll *never know*. I'm going to get us another drink."

The alcohol has started to take effect and I feel looser. I tell myself that Jasper and I absolutely can be the kind of couple that sees each other when we see each other, no plan, spontaneous but in sync. We can meet in exotic locations and pack enough sex into three days to last us months. I'll be divorced soon and that's the perk of shared custody, right? Days to myself and freedom to travel. I finish the rest of my drink before I can admit to myself how tired I am just thinking about it. The picking up and leaving. Making sure everything is covered before I go and then playing catch-up once I'm back. That loose feeling is slipping through my fingers.

"You look troubled." Jasper holds a drink in each hand, looking like he has a delicious secret.

"And you look like trouble."

"How about a special drink."

"How special?"

"Molly special."

"Did you have one?"

"A second ago. You don't have to drink it—"

I down the drink. I want to feel young and carefree like everyone else at the party. I want more shared experiences with Jasper to get us through the inevitable time apart. Jasper's eyes go wide. "Did Santa Fe Diana just emerge from the darkness? L'Wren is going to be very upset she missed this."

I laugh and pull Jasper onto the crowded dance floor. Within minutes, I feel the music coming up through the bottoms of my feet to my head, my scalp tingling. It's the most magical music I've ever heard. Like it was written just for all of us here, at the party. My new friends. The Molly rolls through me and I draw even closer to Jasper like we're in a bubble I don't want to pierce by moving too far away. We exist for each other, I tell myself, as if it's all so obvious. Gratitude overwhelms me and I want to thank him out loud for all the pleasure he's given me. Let him know how meaningful it is and how it has helped me.

"Thank you," I whisper in his ear, our cheeks pressed against each other.

"Always," he answers. It's like he always understands what I'm groping to express, I tell myself, no matter how complex. One song bleeds into the next and we never stop moving, both of us flushed and sweaty. My mind is clear of everything except the sensation of Jasper's touch.

I don't know how long the guy in leather pants and no shirt has been standing there. His pupils are as huge and dilated as ours must be. "I just had to tell you. It's beautiful watching you two. You guys are so in love and I can feel it from across the room. Do you mind if I massage your hand while we talk?"

"Go ahead," I say, like it's the greatest idea ever. I offer him my hand.

"I want to be like you guys when I'm old. Really. You're so beautiful." He kisses each of us on the palm and then disappears back into the crowd. Jasper laughs and pulls me closer. He breathes me in.

I look up at him. The room is on a slight tilt, but the effect is somehow comforting, like this is how the building's architect intended it to be. Jasper tucks a sweaty strand of my hair behind my ear. "Is this real?" I ask him.

"Are we real now?" he asks. "I want us to be real."

"We're real."

He smiles down at me, then lifts my chin and kisses me deeply. "I love you, Diana. I really do."

"This isn't just the drugs?" My thoughts feel so clear but my arms feel like they're suspended in Jell-O.

"Who the fuck cares? Come here." He holds me tightly. "You're incredible. Your face. Your brain. Your legs. Your lips. This is it for me. You are it."

His body feels so good pressed against mine. The pressure of his fingertips against my back. A wave of overwhelming tenderness for him washes over me. "I love you too."

In the morning, everything hurts. My jaw is sore, and I've never been so nauseated in my life. Jasper is fast asleep beside me. It's been three hours since we passed out in each other's arms, after floating back to his hotel room and taking what must have been a forty-five-minute rain shower. We sat on the tiled bench and rubbed each other's feet until the drug wore off. And then I set my alarm for eight thirty. I promised Petra I'd meet her at nine thirty for the photo shoot I've put off twice already. If I leave soon, I'll make it right on time.

Jasper stirs. When I turn my head to face him, the room swims.

"I still feel it. I love you." His voice is heavy with sleep as he curls into me. "It wasn't the drugs. Or the DJ," he teases and pulls my body into his. He kisses my cheek. "I meant what I said last night. We're still real. Still hopelessly in love."

I sit up and steady myself on the edge of the bed and he tilts his face up to me. He's waiting for a response. But I'm scared of our shared declaration last night. I'm frightened by being "real." In the morning light, picturing ourselves fitting into each other's lives feels hard, if not impossible. His suitcase sits on the floor near my feet, half packed. He's leaving town again in two days and coming back when? We move in worlds outside of our bubble that we could never squeeze into a hotel room or three days together. And do we want them to? *Do we have to name it?* I want to ask. Oliver and I never discussed being "real." We just were.

I want to put on the Molly glasses again so I can feel the gratitude, the closeness, the deliciousness of Jasper's skin. He's still as handsome as ever, maybe even more so with his dark stubble and sleep-tousled hair. Maybe the euphoria is still here, just buried underneath the heavy blankets of a hangover.

"Nothing has changed for me either." I pull myself from the bed with a lie, leaving the warmth of his body.

At the studio, everything is loud. In the bathroom, I splash cold water on my face. I look like hell. Everything hurts. I hover over the toilet. Nausea churns inside me in heavy, choppy waves.

Petra knocks on the door.

"I'll be right there."

I rinse out my mouth and open the door—Petra looks perfect and fresh, standing in front of me dressed in a Prada jumpsuit with three-inch Louboutin heels and a fresh blowout. I put a hand to my chest, attempting to cover up the coffee stain on my shirt.

"You didn't forget, did you?"

"I'm ready."

She looks doubtful. "I have one of the best photographers in Dallas behind me, so look alive. She shot my book jacket and she's a genius."

The studio door opens and a four-person crew hurries in. Each one looks past me as they enter the room, unable to imagine that I'm their model for the day.

At some point, Liam appears, takes one look at me, and runs back out for egg sandwiches and Gatorade. "You're going to need this. Drink it." I sit on a chair and close my eyes while I have makeup put on by a kind man who smells like gardenias. "Don't worry, hon. We're going to turn this all around." After the lashes are on, my lips have been lined, and my skin has been evened out with light-reflecting makeup, I come back to life.

"We have three looks," Petra informs me. "One: the shower, fogged-up mirror, wearing only a towel, just got fucked. Two, Met Gala after-party feel, makeup running, just got fucked. Three, sexy girl next door, jeans and a worn-in T-shirt, just got fucked by a neighbor."

"Why am I always 'just got fucked'?"

She waves a hand. "It's just a lazy way to describe the vibe you put out. That's all. Nothing too overt."

"Just a second." I run to the bathroom and dry heave into the toilet. What was I thinking last night? I'm way too old to feel this way.

When I emerge, Petra studies me.

"Big night last night?"

"No, I'm fine."

Petra narrows her eyes. "I'd guess you're pregnant . . ."

"No!"

". . . but you are grinding your teeth. So, yes, must have been a pretty big night."

Surprisingly, Liam is the one who keeps us on schedule, running through each look and carefully monitoring the time, maybe afraid I'll vomit if we go overtime. Kirby keeps us all well fed and happy and Petra tries to put me at ease. As soon as the soft-spoken photographer raises her lens, I feel my entire body stiffen. I can't remember how a woman holds her body, every movement I try is wrong. A deer in headlights. "Let's start with just the face, Diana. It will be a close-up so don't worry about your body. Very small movements. Just put your finger to your lip. Oooh, that's perfect. You're a natural."

After the first hour, I change into the T-shirt and finally start to relax. My hair is tousled—of course it is, because maybe I just got fucked?—but the look feels the most like me. Nothing too constricting so that I can't move like myself and nothing too loose that I worry something will slip out.

For several long minutes, I don't think about posing or the camera. Or about what Oliver would think. Or Jasper. I imagine myself into interviews I've done and into a feeling of confession. I imagine sharing some secret desire I've never spoken out loud and the feeling of lightness that comes after.

"I love it!" Petra can feel it too. A sensuality and freedom emanating from my body.

Without thinking, I pull the T-shirt over my head so that I'm top-less and turn away from the camera, looking over my shoulder directly into the lens.

"Diana. This is it. This is the one."

After the shoot, I race home to meet Oliver and Emmy, still in my hair and makeup.

"Wow," Oliver says. "You look amazing."

"Like an L.O.L. doll," Emmy agrees before running inside.

"I was just about to wash my face."

"Were you at an event?"

"No . . . No . . . I was roped into one of those department store makeovers. The makeup artist went a little crazy." The lies have become second nature.

"You look good."

"Thank you."

"So. I have some news."

"Do you?" *Katherine is moving in. They're engaged. Katherine's pregnant?*

"I sold Frontier Lane for a three-hundred-thousand-dollar profit. Closed this morning."

"Oliver!" I'm flooded with relief—with a side of shame for feeling so relieved. "That's amazing."

"Money will go right back into the savings account. Plus a profit."

"Wow. Congratulations." I think about inviting him in but my head is still pounding. "What will you do next?"

"Find another property, hopefully. Start again. Older and wiser."

"Congratulations," I say again. "That's huge."

"I thought maybe we could go to dinner and celebrate. With Emmy."

"Together?"

"Do you have other plans?"

"No. It's just . . ."

"You're right. Bad idea."

"No. I'm fighting off something." Like a Molly hangover. "I was thinking I'd go to bed early, once Emmy's asleep. But, rain check?"

"Yeah. Of course."

He turns to leave, then pauses. "Diana?" He faces me again.

"Yeah?"

"Is it too much? Everything that's happening in therapy?"

"No . . . I think it's . . . I'm just really tired."

After he leaves, I tally up all the lies I've told today: I lied about coming down with something, when I'm actually hungover. I lied to Petra about my late night, and I lied to Oliver about a photo shoot—a lie of omission, maybe, until I made up the part about being at a makeup counter. I lied about therapy not being too much. I loathe going and it does feel like too much.

And worst of all, the day started with a lie:

I still feel it. I love you. Nothing has changed for me.

Nothing has changed for me either.

We both lied.

Chapter Seventeen

—

"Duly noted." I tighten my grip on the arm of Miriam's couch.

Oliver sighs and tips his head back, staring straight up at the textured ceiling. "Why aren't you taking this seriously? You wanted to come back to therapy and now here we are and you're saying things like 'duly noted'?"

"We're getting a divorce, Oliver. It's a little fucking late for therapy!"

"You agreed!"

"To the divorce or the therapy? Because I'm not sure I agreed to any of it. And now you want to dictate what we talk about."

Miriam interjects. "What would you like to talk about, Diana?"

"You want to talk about our sex lives? Okay." I turn away from him, toward Miriam. "Maybe we should talk about why my husband knew I was faking orgasms but still made love to me the exact same way each time."

"Did it even matter?" Oliver asks.

"Apparently not."

"All I wanted to do was please you. To make you happy. And sex was this constant reminder that I couldn't."

"So say something! You could have talked to me. I was right there."

"So was I."

"Maybe you should have watched a YouTube tutorial." A low blow. Oliver shrinks into the couch. Walk it back. "Or maybe you should have asked the person you were having sex with."

Oliver doesn't fire back. He gets quiet. And then, "I couldn't."

"Why not?"

"I don't know. I already felt like such a failure. Like a bland piece of nothing."

I dig my fingernails into my palms.

"Diana? You look like you want to say something?"

"I want to scream, actually."

"Okay."

"But I can't. Because if I scream, Oliver will feel worse and then we'll both feel worse. This is how it goes. This is why I couldn't ever say anything, because I'll be stuck in the loop of always making Oliver feel worse."

"Oliver? What do you hear when Diana says this?"

He doesn't look at Miriam. He keeps his eyes on me. "You know what I think about all the time? The first time we had sex. In my old bedroom. And I asked you if you came. And you said yes. And a part of me didn't believe you. But it felt like a silly thing to call you out on. And for my own ego, I needed to believe it. But it set a precedent."

I think about that night, too, about how safe I felt with Oliver as soon as I met him. He was so steady when everything else around me was shaky. I was heartbroken and broke and alone in a new city. And the sex between us was tender and it was good but never great and I didn't come. I lied and then I lied again. And then the very things that made me safe, I began to resent him for. My needs changed and so did his—we both knew it and we still couldn't have a fucking conversation about it.

"All I wanted was for you to want me. To really want me. I wanted you to want to rip my clothes off."

"I should have been honest with you," I say.

"What would that have sounded like? You being honest with Oliver?"

I owe him this. I owe him the truth. "We had the same sex for so long. And for some reason it felt wrong to even suggest a different way. I felt dirty. Like I would shock you. Or disappoint you."

"What did you want to do?"

"It's not just a position I wanted to try—it was a feeling, a way we approached it. Sex with you felt old-fashioned. Like you were older than you are. Or younger. One of them."

"I'm not a total prude, Diana. Not like you think."

"But when . . . when you listened to that fantasy . . ."

"What fantasy?" I'm in dangerous territory now and I know it.

"The recording I played for you once, in our bed, when Miriam asked us to share a secret. I played you that recording of a woman talking about sex . . ."

"But that wasn't you talking. It wasn't your fantasy—"

"It could have been! And the look on your face . . ."

"I felt like you set me up on that one. I didn't know what you wanted me to say."

"Maybe not that it was 'creepy'?"

"I never said it was creepy."

"You didn't have to, Oliver. I felt it."

"But that wasn't you!"

I turn to Miriam. *Bingo.* Oliver was fine judging other women. Judging their desires. Their fantasies. It was fine because it wasn't me.

But that only made me want to retreat into my shell even further. What were my fantasies allowed to be? And why did I feel I needed permission? It's as if a version of my desire was cemented long ago and any deviation from it is some kind of betrayal we stumble over or walk the long way to avoid.

I hurry to meet L'Wren at school, straight from therapy. We sit through a long planning meeting in a crowded auditorium of impassioned parents trying to decide what the fall fundraiser should be after a disastrous last-minute cancellation from the golf club that had promised to host a tournament.

It's the ninth volunteer job I've signed up for since school started. At least when the other moms gossip about me and Oliver it will have to include, *You mean Diana who organized the Gardenpalooza? What a shame her marriage didn't make it!*

After lots of hemming and hawing and many bad ideas—the dreaded silent auction; a magic show by the former principal who must be in his nineties; the ever-reliable stinker *Housewives of Rockgate*—one of the dads proposes writing a letter to Cher to see if she will consider performing for the school. L'Wren loses patience and takes charge.

"Let's do a dance, just for the parents. We'll call it 'Party with a Purpose' and it'll be an eighties-style homecoming, so everyone can wear their hair real big and their dresses very short. K?"

After a unanimous vote in her favor, L'Wren walks me to my car. "Jesus. Why can't the parent body just admit they need an excuse to get wasted on a weeknight? Bye, Penny. Sorry they didn't go for your Bluey theme. That would have been a blast." She loops an arm through mine and asks about Jasper. "So y'all will get to see each other before Iceland?"

"He's flying in this weekend and cooking me dinner. Just the two of us."

"At the hotel?"

"No. He booked an Airbnb this time. Just for the weekend."

"That feels like a step in the right direction. Soon it'll be a month-to-month rental, then a lease, then . . ."

"Okay. I get it."

"Too bad he won't be here for homecoming! We could take Jasper and Arthur and really blow up the gossip mill . . ."

When we get to my car, she stops. "I just gotta say again, I'm so glad we are going through this together. I'd be so lost if it was just me and all the other sad, divorced moms. That's not fair. But you know what I mean." In a throaty whisper she adds, *"Penny."*

"Have you told Kevin you're dating?"

"Mmm. Maybe his assistant will do it?"

"L'Wren!"

"What? I would pay her to do it. I mean, she knows him better than anyone. Do you know I sometimes used to wish they were having an affair? I really did. Some days, in the back of my mind I thought, *Wouldn't it be great if he was fucking someone else and I could make a clean break?"* She sighs, her eyes flitting around the emptying school parking lot. "But no. So now we spend all our time dividing up assets and avoid talking about anything personal. There's a house for sale on the corner that Kevin's put an offer on. We're thinking it'll be nice for him to be nearby. Very conscious uncoupling."

"Wow. You guys are really moving fast."

"It's all part of our mediation meetings. Y'all are in mediation, right?"

When I don't say anything, she narrows her eyes. "You've filed papers at least? Diana! What is taking you so long?"

I try changing the subject. "I think that's great for Halston, you being neighbors."

"I actually prefer Arthur's apartment. It's so cozy. And easy to clean. It's just us."

"And how many cats?"

"Seven."

"Oh my god, I was kidding."

"Relax. Only three are permanent. The rest are fosters."

"L'Wren. I don't know if I should steer you away or thank god you found a male version of yourself."

"Two of them are incontinent. You know how big someone's heart needs to be to manually express a cat's bladder in the middle of the night?"

"Pretty big." I open my car door but L'Wren lingers. She bites at her fingernail, then adjusts her purse with nervous energy. "Ever since we got home from Paris, I keep thinking how lucky we are, you and me. We have more story, you know? I felt a little like . . . this was it. This would be my life. Happy but not happy." Her eyes glisten with tears. "I had no idea there was this much more. And the thing is, I want Kevin to find this too. I want him to have an incredible connection with someone and know that the real thing feels so different."

Chapter Eighteen

Jasper's tongue is inside of me, moving rhythmically. I'm on my back, staring at a stain on my ceiling, just beneath Emmy's bathtub. I make a mental note to call the plumber.

It's the second ceiling I've stared at since Jasper came over. First, we had a shower together, and soon we were making out against the sink—the bathroom ceiling was in good condition, just the tiniest beginning of peeling paint in one corner. And now we're naked on the dining room table, Jasper between my legs. I try to concentrate on the pleasure, the feel of his mouth on me, but each time Jasper suggests we move to another part of the house, I lose focus and the good feeling evaporates. "Are you comfortable?" He looks up at me, concerned. "Let's move to the couch. Last time we'll move. Promise."

He takes me by the hand and we sink into the couch. He kisses his way back down my stomach, stopping at the soft skin of my thighs. I tense around him, holding him in place.

"That's it. Right there."

I will not look at the ceiling. I will not add chandelier bulbs to my shopping list.

"Keep going . . ."

Jasper knows I'm close and slips his fingers inside me. When I let out a quiet gasp, he says, "The kitchen. Let's finish there."

"Jasper . . ."

"What? We've never had sex in your kitchen. God, you're perfect. I've never wanted to make anyone come so badly in my life."

"I'm ready . . ."

"Wait. Not yet."

He leads me into the kitchen. He clears the island and picks me up by the hips. "Lie down."

"Jasper. I think I'd like to just be done."

"But you didn't come."

"Won't you want to have sex in the guest room next? We can wait until then."

"I like it." He kisses my neck, down to my shoulder. "I'm getting to know your house."

"You're marking your territory before you leave for Iceland."

"No. I'm enjoying it. It's exciting. Being here. It feels real. Come on, we're not finished." He picks me up and carries me up the stairs to my bedroom. There's a mania to his movements, a desperation. It reminds me of the times I would tell Emmy that we had five minutes left at the playground and she would run furiously to every piece of equipment, trying to get in one last slide or swing. I force the thought from my head. Our time is not running out.

On the bed, we are gentle with each other, our legs intertwined, our bodies pressed together, and we never take our eyes off each other. He brushes my hair from my forehead, kissing every inch of my face as he thrusts deeper inside me and we come together. I could do this for the rest of my life. And that's what makes it so heartbreaking. Our time is measured in work trips and weekends. Never lifetimes.

He kisses my neck, his body curled into mine.

"So that's the home tour." I smile.

"Nice place," he murmurs into my neck.

"Let's take a shower," I propose. "A real one this time."

"Wait. Come here. Lie with me for one more second. I want to show you something."

Jasper disappears, then reappears holding a new camera.

"I shot on it all afternoon."

"But you love your Leica."

"Sure. But not like this. It doesn't even feel like a camera. It feels like an extension of me."

"It feels new."

"I love new."

"I'm new."

"And familiar. In all the best ways." He kisses my fingers. "I know you here. And here. I know you like this . . ."

"Neither of us is exactly the same as before. We're new—this, us—now."

"Yes. So squeaky new I have to fuck you every single way so I remember how perfect you are."

"And then what?"

"What do you mean?"

"After you've fucked me every single way. What happens?"

"I do it again. And again. For the rest of our lives."

"And what if I get sick? Or depressed? Or my teeth fall out?"

Jasper props himself on his elbow, his expression serious. "What is this?"

"Nothing. It could happen."

"Tell me . . ."

"Jasper. I've chased your attention before."

"That was a million years ago. Let's not go backward to some old argument."

"It isn't an argument."

"It feels like one."

"I'm going to shower." I stand but he grabs my hand.

"I want to know every part of you. I want to know what you're thinking and making and dreaming about making. I want to know about your life and your house and I want to know about your daughter and her school and her friends and her art and what she's making and dreaming about making."

I soften. He pulls me gently toward him. "Diana. There's still so much to know . . ." I give in and lie beside him. "Like why exactly your teeth are going to fall out."

I laugh and he rolls onto me, pinning me to the bed. He's ready for round two. But I can't let it go.

"You leave tonight?"

"My flight is at eight. It's not too late. I could put you in my suitcase."

"It is too late."

"Next time then?"

"Sure."

But a sinking feeling has hit us both. He tries to bring us back up to the surface. "What about this summer? We can meet back in Paris? I mean, for longer this time."

"That sounds great."

Summer is still eight months away. Are we both quietly saying, *Maybe I'll see you then?* We lie in my bed, staring up at the ceiling, our arms touching but neither of us saying a word.

I turn my cheek to face him. "Close your eyes."

"Why?" He looks at me to see what kind of game I'm suggesting.

"Jasper." I place my hand over his eyes.

"They're closed, I swear." He holds his hand over mine, his palms calloused and warm.

"What do you see?"

"The last picture I took."

"Tell me."

"You, in a blue dress, in your backyard. You're barefoot. Your legs are bare, too, and you're turned away from me, looking at something in the grass, maybe. Your hand is up near your face, just about to tuck your hair behind your ear."

After a long pause, I slip my hand from his eyes—but he grabs it and holds it to his chest.

"Is that my parting gift?" he asks.

I smile. "You took the picture. It's yours."

"And you're mine?"

"That picture will always be yours. My turn." I grab his hand and place it over my eyes.

He's quiet for a second, like maybe he doesn't want to play anymore. But then he asks, his voice hoarse, "What do you see?"

I close my eyes tighter. "It's not a picture. More like a film?"

"Yeah?"

"Yeah. My subject is too restless to sit still for a photo. He moves around too much."

"I see." Jasper laughs. "He sounds . . . Well, I'm assuming he's gorgeous."

I laugh too. "How did you guess?"

"I can hear it all over your voice."

"He is gorgeous. And I like the way he moves, the way he walks, the way he drifts in and out of a scene. It only makes him . . . better."

It's calm here in my room. Jasper's hand over my eyes. "Is he all alone? In your film?"

"No." I shake my head. "Not always. There's a woman. She comes and she goes, but he never feels alone." I pull his hand from my face and kiss his fingers. "He's happy."

"The blue dress is real. And so is the photo."

"And so is the film. And my fantasy of us."

Jasper takes me in his arms and holds me against his chest. I think about Paris and maybe seeing him there again and maybe not and my eyes well with tears and I let them fall onto his chest.

"I don't get it. Are you broken up?" L'Wren and I collect balls on the tennis court.

"It's our thing. It's the way we are."

"Your thing? Saying goodbye? I don't like it."

"It wasn't designed to be forever."

"Diana. I know. Just because I'm in love doesn't mean I only speak Hallmark—but there's this charge in the air when I'm around you two."

"I'm grateful I got to feel it in my twenties and again in my forties." I am trying to convince myself. I do feel grateful.

"So you would be with Jasper if you could? If the timing was right?"

"Yes."

"But you want to be with Oliver too?"

"No! No. It's not like that."

"Good." The tension drains from her posture. "Because I would literally kill you. I want to celebrate our divorces at the same time. Maybe we should have a party? Isn't that what people are doing now?"

"Why do we have to celebrate anything?"

"So we control the narrative."

"You haven't told Kevin about moving in with Arthur, have you?"

"No. I've been suckered into cochairing the Party with a Purpose and I really need a solid donation and I don't know how he'll take it. That witch Penny always raises so much money. She blew me away in wrapping paper sales last year. I'd love to see her smug face when I raise six figures."

"As long as you're doing it for the right reason."

"You know what I mean."

"So you'll tell Kevin after the dance?"

"Yes. Right after. After I get his check."

"So you're going with Arthur to the dance?"

"No. Yeah. I mean, no. I mean, he's—" She tosses our last ball in the ball hopper. "He's got this thing . . . he's busy."

She's a terrible liar.

"L'Wren, just because I'm single and going solo doesn't mean you can't bring a hot date."

"What? No. It's like a spay-and-neuter convention. He'll be away and I'll be totally on my own. . . . Pinkie swear."

I narrow my eyes, but she refuses to back down. "L'Wren, are you asking me to homecoming?"

"I'll rent us a limo!"

"Fine. But I'm not putting out."

"We'll see." She taps me on the ass with her racket. "I can be very persuasive after a few strawberry wine coolers."

"Should we pick up where we left off last week?" Miriam asks.

When Oliver is quiet, I lie. "I don't remember where that was. But maybe we can start somewhere new? I've noticed picking up Emmy on Sunday nights from Oliver can be a difficult transition and I'm wondering if there's a better way—"

"You said you dreaded having sex with me," Oliver reminds us. "That's where we left off."

"Right."

"Do you want to expand on that, Diana?"

"Well. Oliver already admitted that we were broken. As people. And as a couple. And broken people don't want to have sex with each other. I didn't find Oliver attractive when he was broken."

"I still found you attractive."

"You always wanted to have sex with me. I'm not sure that's the same thing. You would have sex any time of the day. At a funeral. After I threw up. With our daughter in the bed."

"That's not fair—Emmy was a baby . . ."

"Still. I get that *you* could always have sex. But I need more."

"You didn't find me attractive."

"You didn't find yourself attractive."

Oliver quiets. There is truth here.

"It started to feel like a prescription being filled. If your bad mood became so unbearable or you were mopey, I knew having sex would make it easier to be around you. And then when we did have sex, you were completely unaware of my pleasure. It's like it was fine as long as you came."

Miriam takes a note before asking, "Oliver? How do you feel, hearing this?"

"Uncomfortable, I guess. I don't want this to make me uncomfortable. It's one of the reasons we're here. To discuss our sex life. It's what I've been pushing Diana to do. And now, it's making me want to walk out."

"Why do you think talking about this makes you uncomfortable?"

"Do most men in your office enjoy hearing that their wife dreaded having sex with them?"

"You're making yourself into the victim again."

"I'm not. It's just hard to hear."

"Good thing we don't need to talk about it. Like ever again. I mean, why are we torturing ourselves?" I interject.

Oliver presses on. "I don't know. I didn't ever think sex was something I was supposed to talk about."

"Why is that?" Miriam asks.

"It's how I was raised. Sex is something you have but don't talk about. Sex is for making children. Masturbating is a sin. All that shit they tell you . . ."

"How did you feel when you masturbated as a teenager?"

"I didn't."

"Do you now?"

"Yes. Of course. I don't want to be like my parents. I don't want to be like this. I know how old-fashioned it is. You marry the good girl and you fantasize about the other one . . ."

"Who is the other one?"

"Not your wife."

"Did you feel like you could experiment in the bedroom with Diana or was that not allowed?"

"No. We didn't really experiment."

"Diana?" Miriam asks me.

"No. We had sex the same way, mostly," I answer, truthfully.

"Did you enjoy sex with Diana?"

"Sex was sex. It was fine. I thought I enjoyed it. At the time," Oliver admits.

"Why just at the time?"

"Because since we've separated, I've had better sex. Sex that I enjoy more."

"Wow." I can't help myself.

"Don't take that the wrong way."

"How am I supposed to take it?"

"Well, you've been saying you didn't really enjoy sex with me and the truth is, I didn't either. It was fine. But it can be better. I know that now."

"I'm so glad you're having such great sex, Oliver. I am too."

"Good. Because I want you to be enjoying yourself. Sex is a lot better when the woman is enjoying herself."

"Oh, really? Did you just learn that?"

"You would just lie there, Diana. It was like having sex with a pillow!"

"Fuck you! Really. Fuck you, Oliver! I would just lie there because I wanted it to be over."

"I know. You've told me a hundred fucking times how much you hated it. Turns out I can make women come. And it feels fucking great."

"I'm so glad Katherine is having fulfilling orgasms. Please. Tell me more about that."

"I can make her come with my fingers, with my fucking dick, I can even make her come when I fuck her in the ass."

Silence. The air sizzles with the shame of having gone too far. We don't do this. We never fight. We aren't this passionate about anything. The veins in Oliver's neck pulse. His fists are balled and his jaw is tight. We are alive.

"Let's get back on track here. What I hear you saying, Oliver, is that you wish Diana had been enjoying sex with you more because when a woman puts her pleasure first, it becomes more pleasurable for you."

"I just want to talk about it. It's not off-limits. There's no shame. It's our fucking bodies. We were married. I should know every part of her body. Every fucking part and I don't. And I want to."

Want to, present tense. Was that a slip? Didn't he mean *wanted to*? When we were together?

As if picking up on this, Miriam asks, "What would you say to Diana if you could go back in time?"

"I would tell her that I thought of things too. That we could do. Things I never told her."

"You did?"

"All the time. But I kept them in my head. I was even too afraid to masturbate to them. Like I was a deviant."

"What were they?"

Oliver's face turns pink with embarrassment.

"Oliver," Miriam assures him, "a vivid fantasy life is healthy."

Oliver pauses, still unsure.

"I guarantee it isn't anything I haven't heard—that I haven't read about."

Oliver shifts his body on the couch. "I wanted to handcuff you to our bathroom sink. And lock you inside. I wanted you to wear tights with no crotch. I wanted you to be my toy. I wanted to control when you came. I wanted to discipline you."

In an instant, the energy in the room changes.

"Is that something you would have been willing to try, Diana?"

I feel heat rising in my body, blood rushes to my face. "Umm." I clear my throat, trying to match my voice to Oliver's confident desires. "Yes. I would have. I would have liked that."

Chapter Nineteen

—

Even as October wears on, Rockgate is hot and humid. I'm at my desk with the air-conditioning on when Allen pops his head in. "Knock, knock." Just once I wish he'd knock instead of saying "knock, knock."

"Busy?" he asks but doesn't care.

"Always happy for a break. Come on in." My office is so small that any meeting in here feels intimate. I can smell the syrup Allen had on his waffles on his breath. He picks up my framed photo of Emmy at age two and smiles, like he hasn't seen the photo a million times, then sets it down again. "I trust you've seen the latest teardown Oliver is trying to trick someone into buying?"

"I have. Looks promising."

"Really?" He tips back in his chair. "After the first sale, he's encouraged, I suppose."

"He's good at it. He's really happy."

"For now. Let's see what job he decides to try on next week."

"Diana"—Talia stands in the doorway—"you have a phone call from Emmy's school? He says it's important."

By the time I reach the school, speeding the entire way, Oliver is already sitting outside the principal's office. He stands when I rush in and immediately I feel calmer—he's here and so steady and I'm not alone in my worry over Emmy.

"She's fine, Diana. It's her . . . behavior."

Behavior? Emmy? Every parent-teacher conference since pre-K has started with an ode to how well she listens and follows directions, as if she's a gift to her teachers.

Principal Vance opens his door to see us. He has an uncanny resemblance to Santa Claus.

"This is just a check-in. Not an emergency."

"You asked to see us right away."

"Emmy is not in trouble. And neither are you. I don't know who gets more nervous in my office—the parents or the kids. But I've seen it all." He laughs and all I can hear is a full-bodied *ho ho ho.*

I look at Oliver, who is frowning. "We've never had this kind of check-in. So. It feels important."

Principal Vance folds his hands on his desk in front of him. He seems to relish being the only one in the room allowed to be calm, the only one who knows why we're here. "It's such a cliché, I know. But I've been doing this for decades and I have to ask. Is anything going on at home that I should be aware of?"

"Why?" I ask. "Did something happen? In class?"

Principal Vance opens the red folder in front of him and pulls out an 8 x 11 sheet of paper colored on in crayon, but only black crayon. It's a picture of a girl and a car. The girl is in pigtails and is hurtling toward the ground, having just been hit by the car.

"Oh," is all I say.

Oliver holds the drawing in his hands, studies it. "Is that my car?"

I narrow my eyes. "It looks like L'Wren's."

"This was the first red flag."

"There's more? Like this?" I ask.

"Emmy seems increasingly withdrawn this year. She isn't playing with her regular friend group and hasn't been finishing her lunch."

"She's not the best eater," I say. "She never really finishes . . ."

"So I just wanted to have a check-in. We're here for Emmy and we want to do everything we can to make sure she is thriving. As you know, I'm retiring next year and I'm not leaving any student behind. Is there anything I should know that could help me help Emmy?"

Still looking at the drawing, Oliver blurts, "We aren't living with each other anymore. Emmy splits her time between us."

"Okay. That's new information." I catch a tiny, repulsive glimmer of *I thought so* in his twinkling blue eyes.

"Yes," I say. *Yes, Sherlock, you've cracked the case wide open.*

"Has Emmy been talking to anyone about this?"

"Like a therapist?"

"We have. But . . . not Emmy," Oliver says.

"Fine, fine. Well, we do have some resources." He opens a green folder this time and hands us a flier. There's a clip art picture of an ice cream sundae and across the top: *Join the Banana Splits! Every Wednesday! For kids whose parents are divorced or getting divorced!!* I stare at the double exclamation marks. Of all the after-school activities I've pictured for Emmy, this wasn't on the list.

"It's a wonderful club, started by a fellow school parent. Do you know Raleigh?"

I don't have to look at Oliver. I can hear him shift uncomfortably in his chair.

I accept the flier, folding it in half. "Emmy seems fine to us. And we've been watching very carefully for any changes." I feel like a failure even as I say it. Why haven't I noticed any of these changes? Or have I seen them and not wanted to admit it?

"She presents very well. And I'm sure she is fine. But she could be keeping things inside for your sake. Trying to protect you." Oh god, Principal Vance sounds like Miriam, and Emmy is me, misguidedly protecting Oliver's feelings. Now I'm the one shifting in my seat, uncomfortable in my shame.

Oliver walks me to my car and I try not to cry until I get in, but I can't help it—tears spill before I can unlock the door. Oliver pulls me into a hug. "We totally messed her up," I say into his shoulder. "She's barely eating."

"Diana." He pulls back and offers me his baby-blue mono-grammed handkerchief. It's one of the old-fashioned things about him that I miss. "She had like three bowls of Cheerios at my place this morning. That guy is a cheap Santa impersonator who barely knows our daughter."

"You saw it too?"

"Of course I did. He totally leans in. A red vest in this heat? Come on."

I laugh and blow my nose all at once. But my levity is short-lived. Principal Vance has just reinforced my greatest fear. Our damage has damaged Emmy.

"Emmy loves her friends. Why isn't she playing with them?"

"Who knows? Maybe she's sick of them—she has some pretty needy ones. That girl Addie is intense, with her endless annoying names for her stuffed animals."

"You mean Pinkie Pie Sugar Puss?"

"Ugh. Don't remind me."

"But she must be feeling this. We are. It feels huge. Like this massive tsunami that's crashing down on us. Imagine how that feels for a seven-year-old."

"I didn't know that it still felt like a tsunami for you."

"Of course it does. It's awful."

"It is. Awful."

"What if she never has a healthy relationship because of us?"

"Can I tell you one sad thing?"

"What?"

"Don't let it freak you out. I'm only telling you because it was sweet but also kind of heartbreaking."

"Tell me."

"When she was eating her Cheerios this morning—her second bowl, by the way—she ate two Cheerios at a time. Every spoonful was milk and two Cheerios. Each time."

"Why?"

"She said she didn't want them to be alone in her stomach."

"Ohmigod."

"It took her forever, but she did eat three bowls like that."

"God. We couldn't even throw her a therapist of her own. We're leaving her to work through her pain with a bowl of cereal."

"I'll find someone today."

"We cannot mess her up. She's the best thing we've done."

"She's not messed up. She's perfect. And interesting. She will get through this and be stronger for it."

"And what if she's not? What if all this leaves a scar we can't heal?"

"I don't know. But I'm in it with you. You don't have to feel alone in this."

Oliver looks at me—long and meaningful—it's too close, too intense, too tempting to let him comfort me like he used to. I break eye contact. "I have to go. I have to get back to the office."

"Don't go. Not today."

"I have to, Oliver."

"Let's pull Emmy from school. Both of us, right now. We can go to Buc-ee's and then the water park in Waco. To hell with this school. Our daughter is great."

The entire way to Buc-ee's we are accosted by signs telling us we are almost to Buc-ee's. Emmy reads each sign out loud and has done more reading than she has the entire school year. "MEAT GOOD. JERKY BETTER!" "MY OVERBITE IS SEXY!" "THE TOP TWO REASONS TO STOP AT BUC-EES: #1 AND #2."

"What does that one mean?" she asks.

"I think they're talking about the clean bathrooms. You know, what you would do in a clean bathroom . . ."

"Gross."

"You know what sign you don't see?" Oliver offers. "Buc-ee's. Keepin' it classy."

Judging by the packed parking lot, half of Texas has to go #1 and #2. But the bathrooms are clean and the AC blows cold. And everyone greets us with a smile and a pulled-pork sandwich.

Emmy is already running down the aisles, admiring everything from the Buc-ee's saltshakers to the beaver pool floats. "Ahhh. Look at this Buc-ee's lunch box. Can I have it? For school?" As if adding "for school" justifies any purchase.

"Let's look around first, Emmy. There is a lot to see." We leave with three pulled-pork sandwiches, frozen cookie dough that comes in bite-size pieces, extralarge sodas, vintage bottle cap candy, two Buc-ee's stuffies, and a waffle maker.

"I want to stop here again on the way home," Emmy says, guzzling her 110-ounce jug of Fanta.

Forty minutes later I panic that we've missed the exit. The drive is barren and dusty and it's feeling less and less like there is a surf oasis in the middle of . . . Waco? But our GPS tells us to exit so we do. There's not even a stoplight, just a sign.

Apparently surfers from all over the world fly to Waco for the surf park. Is this it? Right in the middle of . . . nothing?

A sign reads FOLLOW THE ARROW and we do, along a dusty road surrounded by farmland and water towers.

When we arrive at the water park, we immediately get it. It's got that lazy seventies feel mixed with an aloha spirit. Everyone shares the same goal: to surf the perfect wave. There's a large man-made sandy shore and an enormous surf "lake" churning out perfect wave after perfect wave. There are food trucks that serve pizza and snow cones. Cabanas line the shore. And set farther back, A-frame surf cabins to rent for the night.

"What's up, little grommet?" A lanky surfer in hot-pink shorts nudges Emmy.

"I think that's you," says Oliver.

"I'm Pops," the young surfer says. "So, who's getting in the water today?"

"Oh, no. We're just watching. We might go in the lazy river."

"I wouldn't do that if I were you. You see people get into the lazy river but you don't see people get out of the lazy river. You know what I mean?"

"What do you mean?" Emmy asks.

"I think he means no one stops at Buc-ee's."

"Exactly," he says. "There's a ton of pee in that thing. But a spot just opened up if she wants to surf the beginner sesh?"

"Yes!"

"Oh, she's never surfed before," I say, worrying Emmy might get hurt.

"No problem. I'll be out there if she needs help. She can totally surf the white wash if she wants."

Emmy sticks out her hand and Pops takes it and they walk off together toward the enormous wave pool.

"We should stop her, right?"

"Does Pops really work here?"

But Emmy looks truly happy. Are these her people? Pops leads a quick and dirty ten-minute beginners course and everyone lies on their stomach and pops up at the same time. Emmy takes to it immediately and the group heads toward the water. Emmy looks back at us, unsure, and it takes everything in my power to give her a shaky thumbs-up.

"Are we really letting her do this?"

"I think so."

And now Emmy is being led face-first into a massive wave-pumping machine. She paddles out to wait in line for the first wave. She's so tiny we can barely see her. The wave machine starts to churn out what seem to be surprisingly large waves, and my stomach lurches. A balding man is pushed into the first set and wipes out three seconds later, his board flying into the air, landing inches from Pops. The second man in line is unable to get up at all, and at this point I get in the water, prepared to rescue Emmy if I have to.

"This is insane. She's not ready for this."

One of a group of bachelorettes in front of Emmy loses her top on her first wave and I officially panic. They can't just expect Emmy to stand up . . .

But there she goes. Hopping up on her board with two feet, knees bent, riding the wave like she's been doing it her entire life. My mouth opens in disbelief. Oliver cheers. Soon we are jumping up and down, holding each other like Emmy just took home a gold medal.

Instead of joining us to celebrate, Emmy paddles back out to get in line for the next wave and we watch her surf the entire hour-long session. My phone has three thousand blurry photos of a teeny tiny Emmy with a huge smile on her face.

"Should we move to Hawaii?" Oliver asks. "So she can train?"

"Clearly."

Pops comes out of the water grinning from ear to ear. "She killed it! Totally shredded." He gives Emmy a high five as I scoop her into my arms.

"What is the highest level?" she asks me, wiping her nose.

"What do you mean?"

"The hardest one."

"Pro. Professional level, I think."

"Sign me up for that one next time," she says and hops out of my arms, walking ahead to get in line for a snow cone.

"Did she just drop the mic?"

"I think so."

Oliver and I smile at each other, basking in the glow of the feeling—our child excelled at something incredibly hard. Her strong legs. Amazing balance. I wish I were so brave.

Emmy doesn't want to leave the resort. She's promised to clean her room and brush her teeth every day and night without ever being told and never lie again for the rest of her life if we can stay *one night*. Pops gets us the last available cabin, right in front of the lake, and we settle in. Our neighbors in the next cabin share their hot dogs and s'mores. They drove all the way from Florida and are thankful for the company. Their sixteen-year-old son Jackson is practicing popping up on his stationary surfboard and graciously gives Emmy a few tips. I watch my daughter, her expression somewhere between glee and concentration.

After dinner, we stand on the shore of the man-made lake looking toward the tiny island in the center that the locals have coined "Lemur Island." Years ago, one abandoned lemur on the island turned to two and multiplied from there.

Jackson shouts out to us from his porch. "They answer you if you call them! Watch!"

He makes an exaggerated lemur call and is met with tiny calls in return.

Emmy all but explodes.

"I want to do it!" She does her best imitation of Jackson's lemur call, crying out into the night, but is met with only silence.

"More guttural. Like this!" Jackson's father calls. The vocalization is impossible to replicate, filled with trills, shrieks, and clicks. The lemurs excitedly reply.

Oliver and I both try but are ignored. Emmy tries again. Only silence.

"Maybe they're sleeping," Oliver offers.

"But they were awake for Jackson!"

"A little louder, Emmy."

We all cry out at once, standing in a line at the water's edge, as a family. A combination of grunts and barks, growing more desperate. *Please wake up, lemurs!* Just as I'm about to play a YouTube recording of a lemur on my phone we get a call back.

Rrrrrclickclickclickerkerkerkerkhooooooooo!

"They heard us!"

"Try again!"

Emmy perfects the sound and this time she's met with a loud chorus of callbacks.

"There you go!"

It feels like we've won. Standing there in a line, our skin still warm from the sun, bellies full of hot dogs, we can pretend to be a family again. All our problems can stay in Rockgate for one more night.

There are two queen beds inside the room, so Emmy and I take one and Oliver takes the other. We use our fingers to brush our teeth with borrowed toothpaste and play a very short round of "Finish the Story." Emmy doesn't even make it to her turn, she's asleep in seconds. Outside, the crickets' singing is loud, and I can hear laughing from a campfire two cabins over. Beside me, Emmy kicks the sheet off her legs and breathes deep and steady and Oliver doesn't make a sound. The AC is working overtime, constantly stopping and starting as if struggling to find its rhythm. It's too hot to sleep.

I creep into the bathroom, careful not to wake either of them, and lie down in the empty bathtub. It's old and heavy, with tiny cracks along the bottom, but its white porcelain is cool against my skin. I pull off my T-shirt and shorts and lie in my bra and underwear, pressing as much of my naked skin against the tub as I can—feeling my temperature drop.

"We could go outside?" Oliver's voice startles me. He stands in the doorway.

"Too many mosquitoes. I just want to lie in this cold tub."

"Can I get in?"

"No way. I don't want your body heat."

"Move over." He climbs in.

For a moment, I think of pulling on my T-shirt, but I'm too hot and tired and he's seen it all before.

He settles in next to me, his head at my feet. "It was a good day."

"We fixed her." I smile.

"She's a happy kid, D. Whatever happens."

"She is happy. And on her way to becoming a professional surfer."

"Right?" We both laugh. Outside, there's a loud clap of thunder and in an instant the humidity that's hung so heavy in the air all day gives in to raindrops. They fall fast, loud, and heavy against the roof. We both instinctually keep an ear out for Emmy, listening for her to stir from the bed, but she stays asleep. I lean back and rest my eyes, listening to the rain.

"So," Oliver says, "how's the guy in your life?"

"What?" I tip my head up, enough to see how he's tried to arrange his face in a casual expression.

"I know you're seeing someone."

"Not really."

"Oh, sorry. Want to talk about it?"

"*No.* We haven't had enough therapy to talk about that."

Oliver laughs.

"And the baroness? How is she doing? She seems great."

"Yes. Turns out I'm not so good at juggling more than one woman."

"But all the sex."

"I admit I went overboard after I moved out."

"And now?"

"Much simpler. Being with one person."

"Do you tie her to the bathroom sink?"

Oliver smiles. "Come on."

"Do you?" I raise my eyebrows.

"No. That was my fantasy for you."

Something passes between us—and we both look away, briefly. The rain is lighter now.

"Well, I hope she's enjoying the new and improved Oliver."

"Am I? Improved?"

"Yes."

"You want to take him out for a spin? The new me?"

"What?"

"I'm kidding." But he doesn't look like he is, at all. His eyes look suddenly very tired. "It's sad," he finally says. "Our divorce."

His words wash over us both. I stay quiet. Oliver takes a deep breath. "Some days I don't know if I'll survive it."

"Oliver." I try to keep my voice light as I poke his chest with my bare toes. "I'm a recently single lady again. Emmy is drawing car wreck pictures. I need you to tell me it's going to be okay."

Oliver holds my foot in his hand, rubbing it gently. The way he used to do for so many years—especially when I was pregnant with Emmy. His hands are strong and familiar.

When he finally meets my gaze, his eyes are wet with tears. And when he smiles, the tears spill down his cheeks. It occurs to me that I haven't seen Oliver cry in years—not since he called his parents to tell them Emmy was here "and she's perfect."

"Oliver?"

He fixes me with his bright blue-green eyes and smiles. "It's going to be okay. We're going to be okay."

Still holding on to me, he leans back, resting his head against the tub and watching the slow, lazy turn of the bathroom's ceiling fan. "Your turn," he says, his voice thick with emotion.

The rain has stopped, the cicadas are singing, the humidity rolling back in as if it'd never been disturbed.

"We're going to be okay."

Chapter Twenty

——

L'Wren pulls up in a bright pink limo and pops her head out of the sunroof—her hair crimped and pulled into a side ponytail.

"You didn't."

"I so did. We're pulling up to the very front and getting out like we own the place."

We walk arm in arm through the front door of the decorated gym—eighties everything. "So much better to be here on our own. Look at all these sad couples!"

"You're a good friend, L'Wren. The best."

"So are you."

"So what are you going to do? Get on the apps? I could ask if Arthur has any friends?"

"I think I'm going to wait a beat."

"Oh. My. God. Oliver is here. Don't look. He's wearing a white tux."

"What? He said he was with Emmy."

"Must have gotten a sitter."

"Wow."

"Fucking Oliver. I wish I could say he doesn't pull that tux off, but he kinda does." Her eyes go wide. "No, Diana. Ignore him. Let's go for the punch. Hopefully it's spiked."

"We're coparenting, L'Wren. I can't ignore him. We're not even legally divorced."

"Hey." Oliver kisses us both on the cheek.

"Hello." L'Wren can't help being polite. "You look handsome."

"I figured I'd come. When would I ever have the opportunity to wear this tux?"

"Have you written a check yet? Diana put a lot of work into this."

"I did. And I got one from my dad too."

"Oh. Well. Good. Shit. The silent auction. Will one of you please bid on the weekend in Telluride at the cabin? That bitch Penny wants it bad. I know it."

L'Wren flits off to find out when the auction starts.

"You look nice." He admires my turquoise taffeta.

"So do you."

A photographer comes by. "Picture?"

"Umm. Sure."

Oliver puts his arm around me and I smile at the camera, unsure what to do once the photographer leaves.

"You didn't have to come to this."

"I wanted to."

"Oh. I can't make therapy on Tuesday. Can we switch it to Thursday?"

"Sure. What do you have?"

Before I can answer he says, "I sound like my parents. None of my business."

The song changes. "Right Here Waiting for You" by Richard Marx.

"Want to dance?"

"Seriously?"

Silence.

"Yeah."

"Okay."

We slow dance. Energy passes through us. I feel like all the blood vessels inside me are about to explode.

"Do you remember our first dance at our wedding?"

"I do."

"You remember that kid who tried to upstage us?"

"Your second cousin. Jeffrey."

"What a little jerk."

"And a horrible dancer."

"We were so much better. But there he was. Sharing the dance floor. We upstaged him in the end. But still."

"That was a good night."

I look up at him and he pulls me even closer. I want to tell him so many things. I want to tell him that there is still hope for us. That by going through hell and back maybe, just maybe, we could emerge stronger. That our spark has not dimmed completely.

"Oliver . . ."

"Yes."

And that's when I see her. Katherine. Wearing a turquoise taffeta minidress, walking over to us with an easy smile.

My hands immediately fall off Oliver's shoulders and drop to my sides. I step away from Oliver as if he was hot to the touch.

"Diana! I was hoping you would be here! Doesn't he look amazing? He was scared it was too much, but I told him it was perfect."

"Yes. He looks great."

"I've been looking everywhere for someone to give this to. I know it's a fundraiser."

"I can give it to L'Wren. She's the chair."

"Amazing. Thank you! You mind if I cut in? I'd love to get in a dance before I turn into a pumpkin. We have to be back by nine, to let the babysitter go home."

"Sure. Of course. You two have fun."

L'Wren appears immediately by my side. "You okay?"

"I just need some fresh air."

"Absolutely. Come on. You look gorgeous and no one is watching."

L'Wren forces open the heavy gymnasium door. "Does she even have a kid at this school? I mean, who hijacks a random school charity? I hate her, right?"

"No, she's actually really nice. And she made a donation." I hand L'Wren the check and her eyes light up.

"Dammit. She is really hard to hate, isn't she?"

"You don't have to hate her."

"She's pretty easy on the eyes too. In a generic way, of course. Like one of those old-school Neutrogena commercials. But you're high fashion all the way."

"L'Wren, I need to tell you something."

"What is going on? What is that face? Are you sick? God. Are you fucking sick?"

"No."

"Emmy? Please don't tell me Emmy—"

"No, no, it's not anything bad. Or, at least, I don't think it's bad." For months I've wondered if L'Wren will think it's wrong. Up until her divorce, she'd been so protective of our lives, keeping us safe in the small bubble of being perfect wives in Rockgate. We lunched at the same places as the other moms, practically wore the same uniform as them, and sat in a line at the same recitals. I learned party tricks like how to share a confession about a "parenting mistake," with no real confession or mistake shared. I read rooms and figured out which pieces of me were too much. But now, standing in front of L'Wren, it all seems like a tiresome, giant miscalculation.

"I've been working on this project and I haven't told you about it. I don't really know why not. It's important to me and I want you to know about it. It's a website called Dirty Diana."

"Dirty?"

"I post sketches and paintings and I interview women about their erotic fantasies and desires. The images of the women represent how they feel, how they look, when they allow themselves to fantasize. I should have told you about it a long time ago. Liam said you would be okay with it . . ."

"Liam?"

"He's been helping me out with the site. He's been great. Really. He's so smart."

"Sorry. Wait. What? You've been employing my stepson for how long? Making . . . erotica?"

"Saying this all out loud, I am realizing what a big mistake it was to keep this from you. Like it's something to be hidden. I was going to tell you in Paris. But I should have told you even before that—"

"How long has Liam been working with you?"

"I don't know. A few months. Alicia and I have been working on it longer."

"Alicia?"

"I underestimated you and that's the worst part."

"Underestimated?"

"And misjudged—"

Her eyes well with tears. "You certainly misjudged Liam. Why not hire him to design a rocket for NASA? I mean, erotica? Diana. Liam used to masturbate to my *Good Housekeeping* magazines. He still giggles at the word *penis* and he walked out of the room when we were watching *Basic Instinct*. So yes, misjudgment all around."

"He's actually been really helpful. Not with content. But he's been so supportive—"

"I'm your friend, Diana. I could have been supportive."

"I know. I'm so sorry, L'Wren."

"I don't want to be mad at you, Diana. I actually really need you."

"I need you too. Can we just reset? Pretend this never happened?"

"But it did happen. I mean, what did you think would happen if you told me?"

"Honestly? I thought you would try to talk me out of it."

"You thought I would try and talk a newly separated mother living in a Texas suburb out of making erotica with my stepson? That's what you thought?"

"Isn't that crazy?" I ask hopefully.

"I don't have a stick up my ass, Diana. I mean, maybe I'll never be the woman who talks freely about their orgasms at the dinner table, but that doesn't mean I'm a nun. You know?"

"I know."

"I can't believe you're making me have this fight with fucking crimped hair." She smiles but I can see by the flush in her cheeks that she's hurt.

"I don't want to fight."

"And I guess Oliver doesn't know?"

I shake my head.

L'Wren sighs. "Piece of advice, Diana? From a friend who's apparently more like the rest of them." She waves an arm toward the school gym. "Maybe you should put a pause on all this. At least until Emmy graduates. Rockgate just isn't ready. And neither is Oliver."

Chapter Twenty-one

—

I FaceTime Alicia. When she sees I'm in bed with the covers pulled over my head, she says, "Hold on." I hear her shout for Nico to make sure Elvis's toast doesn't burn, then she gets into her bed and pulls the covers up too. "Okay. Tell me."

I tell her everything I haven't shared yet—about Waco with Oliver, and our latest therapy, and about the white tux and the dance; about fighting with L'Wren—when I get to this part, I can't help crying. I tell her about how the only place I like to be these days is in the studio, but every time Petra offers to help with Dirty Diana, I push her away.

"What the actual fuck?"

"I don't know. I fucked it all up. I'm so confused."

"Okay. Let's breathe. I learned that at the silent retreat. It cost me twelve hundred bucks for this big takeaway."

We breathe together, in and out, for a long minute.

"All right." Alicia breaks the silence. "Let me tell you what I'm hearing because it's not exactly what you're telling me—"

"You sound like Miriam."

"Thank you. Miriam is clearly a fucking rock star who got Oliver to say he's genuinely sorry and admit he wants to tie you to a sink. And she got you to admit some shit too. Probably long overdue."

"Hello? I'm very fragile, remember?"

"Okay, here's what I'm hearing: Dirty Diana is something you enjoy and you're letting yourself enjoy it. You and L'Wren had your first fight, which will only make you two stronger once you make up. And by the way, we kinda knew that would have to happen one day with how tightly you are *both* wound."

"Still very fragile."

"Oliver's got his groove back, which is turning you on, and I'll need to hear more about that. What you're not talking about is second-guessing saying goodbye to Jasper. Fine. But you're still allowed to miss him like crazy *and* it be the right decision. He was never a permanent solution. Did I nail it?"

"Yes."

"So what is so scary?"

"What about what L'Wren said? About putting everything on pause?"

"Diana. It's Rockgate, not Gilead. And she doesn't really believe that. She's hurt. I get that. Friends hurt each other's feelings sometimes and then the good ones get through it."

"It's just . . . what if—"

"What if people find out you like sex?"

"You know what I mean."

"Are we not supposed to talk about sex? Let me tell you something absolute. You deserve pleasure. You already know that. But you can love sex and you can also dread sex and be bored by it. All of that is fair and normal. You do not owe anyone sex in order to have a happy marriage. Are you writing this down?"

For the next week, I call in sick to work and spend every day at my desk in Petra's office space, beneath the open window. I tore up the sketch of myself and decided to try painting the image in my head instead. I think of Sandrine while I work. Of putting my mostly vulnerable self into the world like she has. So far it's just the outline of my shoulder, which I've started and restarted three times. Petra drifts in and out, always shielding her eyes. "You'll show me when it's done!"

I try calling L'Wren first thing in the morning, then again at lunch, and every day on my drive home. She never picks up or returns my texts. But on Friday, exactly a week after the dance, Liam comes into the office and drops a tinfoil-wrapped package on my table, next to a jar full of unwashed brushes.

When I look up he tells me, "Banana bread from L'Wren."

"For me?" I can't disguise my hope.

"She baked it herself."

"For me?" I ask again.

"Yes. For you."

"Is it poisoned?"

"I don't think so?"

I unwrap it, still warm from the oven.

"It's a good thing," Liam assures me. "I've seen this before. It's L'Wren's way of saying she's working through things without having to say *I'm working through things.*" He helps himself to a thick slice, and I hand him a paper towel to catch the crumbs. "Also, she's letting me stay at the house, even now that Catman is rooming with us. She admitted she likes having me around, and that she's 'fine' with wherever I choose to spend time." Around a full mouth he tells me, "You're like two days away from her fully answering your phone call."

That night, I stay late at my desk working, all alone. I eat most of the banana bread for dinner and paint until my hands ache. For a long while, I stand at the studio's big window and look out over the street. It's late and still and all the storefronts are shuttered. At the end of the block, a tall, skinny man swerves along the sidewalk. He's moving toward my building but stops just short, under the glow of the only streetlight, in front of a rusted station wagon. I watch as he fumbles around in his pants pockets, stopping once to steady himself, his hand pressed to the roof of the car. Stooped like this, he reaches into his coat pocket. This time, he finds his car keys. I think about calling out to him, warning him that he's in no condition to drive. But then, the keys slip from his fingers and clatter to the ground. The man gets on his knees. He gropes along the dark pavement for a long time, then finally gives up and makes his slow, swerving way back to his feet. Standing upright, he shudders and for a second I think he might get sick. Instead he takes a long stride, then another, and disappears down the sidewalk. I exhale, fogging the glass, unaware I was holding my breath.

"Close one." I jump at the sound of Petra's voice.

"Sorry," she says. "I thought for sure you heard me come in."

"I got a little transfixed." I blush, as if I've been caught reading something I shouldn't. "What are you doing here so late?"

Petra purses her lips. "Honestly? I had a feeling you'd be done."

I follow her gaze to the canvas. "Oh. Almost." I'd finally finished my shoulder and then moved on to my torso, then hips and legs, painting myself seated on the edge of a bathtub. I'm happy with my face in profile, but the hands are all wrong. "I want to add some shadow, near my wrist—"

"It's perfect, Diana." Petra squeezes my fingers in hers. I rest my head on her shoulder and stay there.

. . .

I sleep curled up on the love seat. I thought about driving home but could barely keep my eyes open. And I felt a strange pull to stay close to the painting until it was dry enough to move or at least until it wasn't so dark and quiet in the office. I told myself I'd take a quick power nap—and then I didn't open my eyes again until the late-morning sun was streaming through the windows.

On the drive home, I feel lighter. I imagine this is the way Oliver felt when he quit working for his dad. I imagine him driving home, his shoulders finally relaxing, his breath coming slower and steadier with every mile between him and the office.

As I get closer, I steel myself for the quiet house and the hours to fill before Emmy comes home from a Saturday with her grandparents. But when I pull into the driveway, the house isn't empty. Oliver is in the front yard, planting flowers in the unseasonably hot autumn sun.

He has his headphones in and is so focused on pushing a wheelbarrow of soil, he doesn't notice my car. I stay behind the wheel. I watch as he packs dirt into the flower beds. His shirt is soaked with sweat and I can see the outline of his muscled back. Every few seconds, he brushes the hair from his eyes with the back of his work glove. For a brief second I allow myself to imagine he's still my husband and I am coming home to him. In my daydream, there is no lingering tension, no hangover of a hundred fights—he's happy to see me and that's it. I shut off the car. He still doesn't see me. My heart races as I tuck the fantasy into the smallest corner of my heart, taking up a space so small that nothing can break.

"Oliver?" I don't call loudly but he looks up. "What are you doing?"

He turns off his music and stands. "Planting zinnias. Up the walk, like you always wanted." He's slightly out of breath. "I was going to plant roses, too, but then I remembered our night at the hotel fiasco . . . and thought better of it."

"It's ninety degrees out."

"I'm almost finished." He takes out his baby-blue handkerchief and wipes the sweat from his forehead.

"Why?" I haven't lifted a finger, but suddenly I feel out of breath, too, a ring of brightly colored flowers around me. "Why are you doing this?"

Oliver's eyes are serious and sparkling. "Isn't it obvious?"

He closes the space between us.

"No." My voice shakes, but when he takes both my hands in his I say, "Tell me."

Oliver leans in and whispers in my ear, the feel of his breath on my neck sending an electric shiver through my body. "Because I want to handcuff you to the sink."

Acknowledgments

—

All of our colossal thanks to:

Our dream editor, Whitney Frick. Whit, remember when we pitched you a felonious mother and . . . murder? (We do!) Thank you for always guiding us—and *Diana*—from the edge, with wisdom, grace, and confidence.

To Anna Worrall and Alia Hanna Habib. This book would not exist without your advocacy. Thank you for so wholly looking out for us, while also keeping approximately sixty-three different schedules straight. Thank you to the entire Gernert Company, with a huge thank-you to Sophie Pugh-Sellers, Ellen Goodson Coughtrey, and Rebecca Gardner.

To the incredible Dial/Penguin Random House team. We are so grateful to be on this adventure alongside you. A special thank-you to Talia Cieslinski, Debbie Aroff, Avideh Bashirrad, Vanessa DeJesus, Corina Diez, Laurie McGee, Michelle Jasmine, Cassie Gonzales, and Donna Cheng for all the care you've shown us and these books.

To Rocio Montoya. Thank you for bringing Diana to life in such a dazzling way.

To Amanda Hymson, the best film agent a girl could have; and to Sean Marks, the most loyal lawyer in the business.

To Kate Meltzer. Thank you for an illuminating and dreamy trip through Paris.

To Lynette Howell, Beau St. Clair, Jenno Topping, Pam Abdy, Stephanie Savage, Tracy Falco, Effie Brown, Alex Saks, and Bea Sequeira, truly courageous and hardworking champions of women.

To Marie Lu and Melissa de la Cruz, trailblazers and friends, always.

And to our big, beautiful families. Thank you for putting up with our doubts, deadlines, and fewer showers. We love you.

Lifelong best friends JEN BESSER and SHANA FESTE met as eleven-year-olds in California and have been collaborating ever since. *Dirty Diana,* first launched as a podcast starring Demi Moore, debuted at #1 on Apple, was nominated for Podcast of the Year, and won the Ambie for Best Fiction, Screenwriting. Shana is the award-winning screenwriter and director of several feature films, including *Country Strong* and *Run Sweetheart Run.* Jen is a fiction editor and publisher. They now live thousands of miles apart and talk every day.

ABOUT THE TYPE

This book was set in Dante, a typeface designed by Giovanni Mardersteig (1892–1977). Conceived as a private type for the Officina Bodoni in Verona, Italy, Dante was originally cut only for hand composition by Charles Malin, the famous Parisian punch cutter, between 1946 and 1952. Its first use was in an edition of Boccaccio's *Trattatello in laude di Dante* that appeared in 1954. The Monotype Corporation's version of Dante followed in 1957. Though modeled on the Aldine type used for Pietro Cardinal Bembo's treatise *De Aetna* in 1495, Dante is a thoroughly modern interpretation of that venerable face.

Books Driven by the Heart

Sign up for our newsletter and find more you'll love:

thedialpress.com

 @THEDIALPRESS

@THEDIALPRESS